Beaver's back!

HERE'S BEAVER!

Beverly Cleary

**Based on the television series
created by Joe Connelly
and Bob Mosher**

WILDSIDE PRESS

HERE'S BEAVER!

BEAVER, THE MAGICIAN

Beaver Cleaver, whose real name was Theodore, was a medium-sized boy with brown hair that fell over his forehead who always wore a baseball cap outdoors and also wore it indoors when his mother was not looking. He lived with his mother and father and older brother Wally in a stone-and-clapboard house in the medium-sized town of Mayfield. Beaver liked things the way they were, but right now that was his problem.

If there was one thing Beaver did not want to do it was spend his spring vacation in another town with his Great-aunt Martha. Not that he did not like Aunt Martha. He did like her. She was a nice old lady who believed in baking plenty of cookies for boys to eat between meals. It was just that he did not want to spend spring vacation with her when there were so many interesting things he could do with Larry and Whitey and the rest of his friends. Maybe they could start a secret club or practice baseball or . . . well, there were lots of things boys could find to do when their day was not interrupted by school.

At Aunt Martha's house Beaver would have to stay clean all the time and remember his manners and be shown off to a lot of other old ladies who would be sure to talk about which side of the family he took after. They would drink tea out of flowery little cups and argue politely about whether he had his mother's eyes and his father's ears and all the time he would want to be back in Mayfield getting dirty with the other fellows who didn't care whether he minded his manners or not.

No, Beaver did not want to go visit Aunt Martha and that was why he and Larry Mondello, the fat, good-natured boy who was almost his best friend stopped at Uncle Artie's Magic Shop on the way home from school. Beaver hoped that by staying out of sight as much as possible his mother somehow might forget about sending him to visit Aunt Martha.

"Hey, I know what," said Larry as he pushed open the door of the magic shop. "During spring vacation we can practice up on a whole bunch of magic tricks—you know, get really good and when school starts we can have a lot of fun fooling all the kids."

"That's a keen idea," agreed Beaver, forgetting Aunt Martha in the fascinating jumble of Uncle Artie's Magic Shop and thinking what fun it would be to fool the whole fifth grade.

Inside the shop tricks and games and gadgets were everywhere. A boy could spend a week in here and not look at the same trick twice. Uncle Artie nodded to the boys as they entered and went on about his business. That was one of the reasons

Beaver liked to come here. Uncle Artie always let boys poke around his shop all they wanted, and when Beaver grew up he wanted to have a magic shop of his own exactly like this and let boys enjoy themselves without bothering them, too.

When Larry wasn't looking, Beaver picked up a rubber witch's mask with warts and crooked teeth and slipped it over his head. He sneaked up behind Larry and tapped him on the shoulder.

Larry looked around and laughed. "Hey, Beaver, I didn't know you were so good-looking." As Beaver pulled off the mask Larry held up a rubber bug. "Let's buy some of these and scare girls with them."

Beaver did not think this a good idea. "Why buy rubber bugs when we can scare girls with real bugs?" Scaring girls was too easy. He wanted to do real tricks, sleight of hand and things that real magicians did. Maybe even sawing ladies in two.

"Yeah, that's right," agreed Larry, picking up what looked like a wand. "No use wasting money on rubber bugs when we can get real ones free. How about buying this instead?"

"What is it?" asked Beaver.

"I don't know," admitted Larry. "Maybe it squirts ink or something." He held the wand out toward Beaver and suddenly a bunch of flowers popped out.

"Hey, that's neat!" Beaver was enthusiastic. "Hey, Uncle Artie!"

"Yes, boys?" said Uncle Artie.

"How much is this?"

"Only three-fifty," said Uncle Artie.

"No, I guess not," said Beaver reluctantly. It would have been fun to wave a wand at his mother and produce a bunch of flowers. No, not his mother. The sight of flowers might make her think of Aunt Martha's hats and Aunt Martha's hats would make her think of sending Beaver to visit Aunt Martha.

"Say, Larry," said Uncle Artie, "don't you feel uncomfortable with that egg behind your ear?"

"What egg?" asked Larry.

"This egg right here," said Uncle Artie as he reached over and took an egg from behind Larry's ear.

"I'll bet you had it in your hand all the time," said Beaver who could not help being impressed.

Uncle Artie waved his hands. "Mumbo . . . jumbo . . . squigglety!" His hands were empty.

"That's a neat trick," said Beaver, thinking what fun it would be to pull eggs from behind the ears of his friends at school. "How do you do it?"

"All you have to do is find a boy with an egg behind his ear," said Uncle Artie. "See. Like this." He removed another egg from behind Larry's ear and laid it on the counter. "How about this one?" he asked, picking up two interlocked rings. He put them behind his back, said, "Presto . . . squigglety!" and brought them out separately.

"Boy, how much is that?" asked Larry with enthusiasm.

"Only five ninety-eight," answered Uncle Artie.

"That's kind of more than we've got to spend," confessed Beaver. "Between us we've got fifteen cents."

"I see . . . How about this?" The boys watched while Uncle Artie picked up a small slab of wood and laid a penny on it. His hand slid the wood. He slid it again and the penny had disappeared.

Beaver and Larry exchanged a look of agreement. "We'll take it," said Larry.

"Wait a minute, Larry," said Beaver. "If we spend the whole fifteen cents, we won't have a penny to put in the slot."

"That's easy," said Uncle Artie. "I'll just make you a penny." He slid the wood, produced the penny and handed the boys the trick for which they gave him their fifteen cents.

"You can have dibs on it first, Beaver," said Larry as the boys left the shop. "Then I get to use it."

"O.K.," agreed Beaver who was eager to try their trick on someone. "Hey, instead of a penny, we could do the trick with a dime."

Larry did not agree. "What if you disappeared it and you couldn't get it back? Then you'd be out a whole dime."

Beaver decided Larry was right. A penny was all he cared to risk. When the boys reached the Cleavers' house they found Mr. Cleaver unloading groceries from the car. "Hey, Dad, you want to see some magic?" Beaver asked eagerly. He ran up to his father and made the penny disappear. Then he said, "Mumbo . . . jumbo . . . squigglety," and the penny reappeared. The trick had worked. Beaver had started his career as a magician.

"Well, Beaver, that certainly is a piece of magic you have there, isn't it?" remarked Mr. Cleaver as he lifted a box of groceries out of the trunk of the car.

Beaver was disappointed in his father's reaction. He had expected something different—surprise or even admiration. "Aw, Dad—you know the trick."

"I was a kid once myself, you know," said Mr. Cleaver as he carried the groceries into the house.

"Let's find Wally," suggested Larry.

The boys found Beaver's older brother in Mr. Cleaver's study, where he was looking up something in the encyclopedia. Wally, who went to high school, always had a lot of homework. "Hey, Wally, want to see a trick?" Beaver asked eagerly and performed his trick without waiting for an answer.

"You mean that trick?" asked Wally.

"Yeah, that's the trick." Beaver was crestfallen. He had expected more interest from Wally. "Come on, Larry, let's try Mom."

Mrs. Cleaver was easily found because she was running the vacuum cleaner in the living room. When Beaver offered to show her the trick, she turned off the vacuum cleaner and watched. "Isn't that nice?" she said when Beaver performed the trick.

"I can bring the penny back," said Beaver hopefully.

"Fine. I don't want you being careless with money," said his mother. "And, Beaver don't run off. I want you to take a bath before supper so you will be nice and clean when you go to Aunt Martha's. Your father is planning to leave as soon as we eat."

Aunt Martha's. For a few minutes Beaver had

forgotten. "Aw, Mom—" he began. "Do I have to—"

"Yes," said Mrs. Cleaver, turning on the vacuum cleaner.

Completely disheartened Beaver led Larry outside where the boys sat down on the front steps. Nobody would get excited about their trick and Beaver had to leave for Aunt Martha's right after supper. Nothing was turning out right today. They sat in forlorn silence, too discouraged to say anything to one another. Some days were like that.

And then Benjie Bellamy, the four-year-old boy who lived across the street came walking across the lawn pulling a little wagon and carrying a tin can in his hand. "Hello, Beaver . . . Hello, Larry." Benjie always liked to tag along after the older boys.

"Hi, Benjie," said Beaver glumly.

Larry was equally glum. "What are you doing with that can?"

"Catching ants," answered Benjie.

"What do you catch ants for?" asked Beaver.

"I talk to them," explained Benjie.

Suddenly Beaver brightened. "Hey, Benjie—you want to see some real neat magic?" He wanted to fool *somebody* even if it was only Benjie and if he wasn't good enough to fool a four-year-old who talked to ants he might as well give up.

"Real magic?" Benjie was properly awed.

"Sure," said Beaver. "See this penny? Now watch. I'm going to make it disappear. Watch. Mumbo . . . jumbo . . . squigglety."

"Boy!" Benjie was even more awed.

"Now make it disappear back," said Larry.

"Squigglety . . . jumbo . . . mumbo." Beaver showed Benjie the penny. He could not have asked for a better audience.

"How do you do it, Beaver?" Benjie asked as if he still did not quite believe what he had seen. He looked almost frightened by the magic that had taken place before his eyes.

"Magicians aren't supposed to tell how they do stuff, Benjie," said Beaver, feeling pleasantly superior.

"Yeah, Beaver and I could make his whole house disappear if we wanted to," boasted Larry.

"Let's see," said Benjie eagerly.

"Well, we can't do it now on account of my Mom and Dad are in it," explained Beaver.

"Yeah, and Beaver needs them for later on," added Larry.

"Hey, Benjie, you wait here a second while I go get something and we'll show you another trick," said Beaver. "Come on, Larry."

"What are we going to do?" asked Larry.

Beaver whispered his plan to his friend and in a moment the two boys returned with a blanket. They led a wide-eyed Benjie, still pulling his squeaky wagon, around to the back yard where there was a woodbox set against the garage. Larry took the blanket from Beaver and said, "Now watch, Benjie. I'm going to make Beaver disappear with magic and turn him into a rock."

"That's right," agreed Beaver. "He's going to hocus-pocus me."

Benjie watched fascinated and a little frightened while Beaver stood in front of the woodbox.

"Are you ready?" asked Larry in what was intended to be a spooky voice.

"I'm ready," answered Beaver, trying to sound like a ghost.

Larry held the blanket up in front of Beaver. "Mumbo . . . jumbo . . . squigglety!"

Behind the blanket Beaver quickly opened the woodbox, laid a rock on the ground, climbed into the box and closed the lid.

"Alacazam!" shouted Larry yanking away the blanket with a flourish. "Beaver is a rock!"

Benjie stared fascinated at the rock. "Is that Beaver?"

"Sure." From inside the box Beaver could tell Larry was trying not to laugh. He could hardly keep from laughing himself. He heard Benjie say, "Change him back."

Larry was still struggling to speak seriously.

"You want me to change him into a stick or something first?"

"Uh uh . . . change him back to Beaver," said Benjie.

Beaver heard Larry say, "Well, O.K. . . ." and he was waiting for Larry's signal to tell him to come out of the woodbox when he heard his mother's voice calling, "Larry! Larry, are you out there?"

"Yes, Mrs. Cleaver," answered Larry.

Beaver heard his mother say, "Your mother called, Larry, and said you were supposed to be home an hour ago."

"Gee, I forgot . . ." was Larry's answer. "Thank you, Mrs. Cleaver."

Beaver waited for the signal to come out. Instead he heard Larry's footsteps going down the driveway.

"Aren't you going to change Beaver back?" called Benjie and inside the box Beaver had to hold his hand over his mouth to keep from laughing out loud.

"I can't," answered Larry who by now had reached the sidewalk. "I am going to catch it when I get home."

In a moment Beaver heard the squeak of Benjie's wagon on the driveway and when he raised the lid of the woodbox and peeked out, Benjie was gone. So was the rock. Grinning to himself because at last he and Larry had found someone they could really fool with magic, Beaver went on into the house where his mother promptly ordered him into the bathtub.

After an early supper Mr. Cleaver drove the reluctant Beaver to his Aunt Martha's to spend spring vacation. There was nothing Beaver could do about it and as he and his father drove through the twilight Beaver began to feel sorry for himself. First nobody in his family would be impressed by his magic and now, cruel and heartless, they were sending him off to his Aunt Martha's where he would have to be clean and polite while they stayed home having a good time. Well, he would fix them. He would think up the best magic trick in the whole world and would baffle them all. Then they would see who could do magic.

The next morning when Beaver woke up in Aunt Martha's spare bedroom, a room that was full of ruffles and—well, *pretty* things that would be easy to bump into and break, he was still feeling cross with his family for spoiling his spring vacation. As he dressed he could picture his mother and father and Wally eating hotcakes in the kitchen and then his father would go play golf and Wally would go play baseball with his friends . . . Everybody but Beaver would have a good time. It wasn't fair. Beaver wished he knew some magic that would whisk him home. That was the kind of magic trick he needed.

The rest of the Cleavers, however, were not eating hotcakes as Beaver pictured.

To begin with, Mr. Cleaver was tired from his long drive to Aunt Martha's and back the night before and so he and Mrs. Cleaver slept later than usual. They were still asleep when the sound of the front door chimes woke Mrs. Cleaver who called drowsily, "Wally, would you go see who it is?"

Wally, who was only half-awake himself, called out, "O.K., Mom," pulled on his bathrobe and sleepily made his way downstairs to open the front door. He was confronted by Mrs. Bellamy, Benjie's mother, whose lips were pinched together in a straight line and by Benjie who was holding a large rock.

"Uh . . . hello, Mrs. Bellamy," said Wally, wondering why she looked so grim.

"Wally, I wonder if you would ask Beaver to come to the door so Benjie can see him," she said.

Baffled, Wally said, "I am sorry but the Beaver isn't here, Mrs. Bellamy."

"See! I told you!" Benjie looked as if he were about to cry.

"Who is it, Wally?" Mrs. Cleaver called from upstairs.

"Mrs. Bellamy," Wally called back.

"I *told* you the fat boy said jumbo jumbo squigglety," said Benjie tearfully.

"Where is Beaver?" asked Mrs. Bellamy.

"He went to visit his Aunt Martha," said Wally who was still puzzled as to what this was all about.

"No, he didn't!" contradicted Benjie. "He turned into a rock."

Then Mrs. Cleaver came down the stairs in her bathrobe. "Why, good morning, Mrs. Bellamy," she said, trying to smooth her pretty blond hair with her hands.

"Mrs. Cleaver, would you please tell Benjie what has happened to Beaver?" asked Mrs. Bellamy.

"Why . . ." Mrs. Beaver plainly did not understand what this was all about. "He's gone to spend spring vacation with his Aunt Martha."

"No," said Benjie. "He's a rock."

"Now listen to me, Benjie," said Mrs. Bellamy carefully. "You just heard Mrs. Cleaver say that Beaver has gone to visit his aunt."

Benjie hugged his rock and said stubbornly, "No. This is Beaver."

By this time Mr. Cleaver wearing his bathrobe had joined the group in the front entrance. "Suppose you come in, Mrs. Bellamy, and tell us what this is all about," he suggested, looking as if he were not quite awake.

Mrs. Bellamy sat down and said to her son, "But Mrs. Cleaver is a big grown-up lady. She wouldn't tell fibs to a little boy."

"This is Beaver," repeated Benjie, laying the rock gently on a chair.

Mrs. Bellamy looked helplessly at the sleepy Cleavers. "I just don't know what to do. He has scarcely slept a wink all night."

"Uh . . . suppose you begin at the beginning and tell us all about it," suggested Mr. Cleaver gently and stifled a yawn.

"Well, it seems that Beaver and some other boy told Benjie that they were going to transform Beaver into a rock and as far as Benjie is concerned, they did it," said Mrs. Bellamy.

"I *saw* them," said Benjie.

"Is that . . ." began Mr. Cleaver, indicating the rock.

"Yes," sighed Mrs. Bellamy. "He thinks that is your son."

Benjie picked up the rock and handed it to Mrs. Cleaver.

"Why . . . uh . . . thank you, Benjie." Mrs. Cleaver sounded as if she were not sure she wanted to hold the rock.

"Benjie, I want you to listen to me," Mr. Cleaver spoke slowly and distinctly. "Beaver's mother and I would be very worried if we thought someone had turned Beaver into a rock, wouldn't we?"

Benjie nodded.

"But we're *not* worried," continued Mr. Cleaver. "Do you know why?"

Benjie shook his head.

"Because we know exactly where Beaver is!" said Mr. Cleaver.

"Me, too," said Benjie, pointing to the rock on Mrs. Cleaver's lap.

Mrs. Bellamy lost her patience. "Benjie, do you want to go without television for a whole week?" she demanded.

Benjie shook his head.

"Then stop saying that rock is Beaver!" his mother snapped.

Benjie looked at his mother so reproachfully that she relented. "I'm sorry." She turned apologetically to the Cleavers. "I thought maybe a little firmness would work. I've tried everything else."

Mrs. Cleaver held up the rock. "Benjie, exactly *how* did the boys turn Beaver into this?"

"First they changed a penny and then they changed Beaver," answered Benjie.

"Benjie, how would you like to talk to Beaver?" asked Mr. Cleaver who looked as if he wished he had a cup of coffee. Mr. Cleaver was one of those grownups who was never completely awake until he had had his coffee.

"O.K.," agreed Benjie.

"Fine," said Mr. Cleaver. "That is exactly what you are going to do." He went to the telephone and started to dial.

Meanwhile Benjie walked over to Mrs. Cleaver,

picked up the rock, turned it over and put it back in her lap.

Mrs. Bellamy looked embarrassed. "I think you had Beaver upside down."

Wally wished Mrs. Bellamy would take Benjie and go home. He wanted his breakfast.

Meanwhile, at Aunt Martha's house, Beaver was dutifully eating the oatmeal that Aunt Martha thought all boys should eat for breakfast and thinking of the fun everyone must be having at home . . . Larry and Whitey thinking up magic tricks . . . Wally playing baseball with the fellows . . . his father getting ready to play golf . . . And here he was, stuck with a big bowl of oatmeal. Some spring vacation!

And then the telephone rang. Aunt Martha answered it and Beaver heard her say, "Why, of course, Ward. He is right here enjoying a nice bowl of oatmeal. I'll call him." She turned to Beaver. "It is for you, Theodore."

Surprised that his father was calling long distance so soon, Beaver picked up the telephone. "Yes, Dad?"

"Hi, Beaver," he heard his father say in a worried voice. "I don't have time for a long explanation, but I want you to say a few words to Benjie Bellamy . . ."

"Gee, Dad, how come?" asked Beaver.

"He thinks you were changed into a rock and I want him to know that you weren't," answered Mr. Cleaver.

"Huh?" said Beaver as he heard his father say, "Here, Benjie, Beaver wants to talk to you."

Beaver heard someone breathing into the telephone. "Hi, Benjie?" he said doubtfully because he still did not understand what this was all about.

"Hi, Beaver," answered Benjie with his mouth too close to the telephone.

Beaver held the receiver farther from his ear.

"Uh . . . how are you?" He did not know what else to say.

"Fine," said Benjie.

"Well . . . uh . . . so am I," said Beaver.

"O.K.," said Benjie.

Beaver could see that this conversation was not going to lead anyplace. "Yeah, well . . . uh . . . goodby, Benjie." He heard a clattering sound and guessed that Benjie had laid the telephone on the table. He strained to hear what was happening at home.

Beaver heard Mrs. Bellamy say, "There! *Now* do you understand that Beaver was never turned into a rock, Benjie."

"Nope," answered Benjie.

"But you just talked to him," said Mrs. Bellamy.

Then Beaver heard his father speak. "Don't you believe that was Beaver's voice you just heard?"

"Sure," was Benjie's answer.

"Then where do you think he could be?" Beaver heard his father ask.

"In heaven!" answered Benjie.

"Oh, dear!" Mrs. Bellamy sounded terribly distressed.

Boy! thought Beaver, pressing his ear against the telephone. Maybe he even thinks I'm wearing a white nightgown and playing a harp. That was one magic trick that had worked better than he and Larry had expected.

Then Beaver heard Wally speak. "I know!" Let's get Larry over here and have him show Benjie how they worked the trick," said Wally. "Hey, look, Benjie forgot to hang up when Beaver did."

There was a slam and Beaver knew that Wally had hung up. He sat staring at the telephone, feeling the way he did when he read a continued story in a magazine. Just when things were getting good he had to wait until the next installment to find out what happened, only in this case he would have to wait until the end of spring vacation. But to have Benjie think he was in heaven . . . Maybe the trick had been *too* successful.

"Was something wrong at home?" asked Aunt Martha anxiously.

"Not exactly." Beaver did not know quite how to explain the situation. "There is this little kid who seems to think I'm in heaven."

Aunt Martha smiled lovingly at Beaver. "You must have told him very nice things about your visits to my house. I think that is very sweet of you."

Beaver decided he had better keep still. He went on eating his oatmeal and wished more than ever that he was home. He would certainly like to listen to his family explain to Benjie that he was not in heaven.

This time it was Wally who was trying to do the explaining. He telephoned Larry Mondello who came running over to find out what was happening. When the situation was explained, he told Wally how he and Beaver had performed their magic trick. Wally found a blanket and everyone trooped out to the backyard to the woodbox. Benjie insisted on bringing the rock so Beaver would not get lonesome.

Wally held up the blanket. "O.K., Larry . . . you watch, Benjie." Larry stepped behind the blanket. "Now it looks like Larry is gone, huh, Benjie?"

"Yeah," answered the wide-eyed Benjie.

Wally removed the blanket. Larry was gone and in his place was a rock.

Benjie looked scared. "Change him back!"

"O.K., come out of there, Larry," directed Wally and Larry, grinning, pushed open the lid of the woodbox. Wally was glad to see Benjie begin to smile. "Now do you see how they did it?" he asked.

"Sure . . ." said Benjie.

"It is just a trick, isn't it?"

"Sure . . ." Benjie picked up his rock and handed it to Wally. "Now make it into Beaver."

"Oh, my." Mrs. Bellamy sounded very, very tired.

Mr. Cleaver stepped forward. "Now, see here, Benjie," he said gently. "He can't turn the rock into Beaver because Beaver is at his Aunt Martha's."

Benjie began to cry.

"Well, I can see there is only one thing to do," said Mrs. Cleaver. Her hair was not combed, her family was hungry, Benjie and his mother were unhappy. This had to stop.

And so for the second time that morning Beaver heard his Aunt Martha's telephone ring.

"Hello?" Aunt Martha seemed to be listening to a long speech about something. "Oh . . . oh? . . . oh

. . . Well, I must say I never heard anything like this. Why doesn't someone go to that boy and say, 'Look here, little fellow, we won't have any more of this nonsense about Theodore being a rock'?"

Beaver listened with interest. Apparently Benjie still thought he was floating around in heaven.

Aunt Martha continued to speak crisply as if she did not approve of what was going on. "Well, all right, June. But in my day, our parents told us what to think and what not to think. Goodby, June." When she had hung up she turned to Beaver. "I just don't understand young folks these days. Your mother says you are to take the first bus home and all on account of a little boy who is full of some nonsense about your being a rock."

"Gee, Aunt Martha . . ." Beaver suddenly felt as if he had been rescued.

"I know," said Aunt Martha sympathetically. "It is a shame you have to cut your vacation short, but I guess you have to do what your mother tells you to. Now you run along and pack your bag and I'll wrap up some cookies for you to eat on the bus."

"Sure, Aunt Martha." Boy, oh boy! Would he ever pack in a hurry!

Two hours later Beaver was met at the Mayfield bus station by his family, who had finally managed to get dressed, Mrs. Bellamy and Benjie who was still carrying his rock. "Go ahead, Beaver," said Mr. Cleaver wearily. "Tell Benjie you aren't a rock."

"I'm not a rock, Benjie," said Beaver.

Benjie looked at the rock and then looked at Beaver while everyone waited.

"Benjie . . . uh . . . Larry and I don't really know how to change kids into rocks or anything," said Beaver.

"I know," agreed Benjie. "You climb into that woodbox."

"Well, gee whiz!" exclaimed Wally. "If you knew how they did the trick, how come Beaver had to come home?"

"I *used* to not know it," was Benjie's explanation.

"Well, thank goodness, that's over!" exclaimed Benjie's weary mother. "And after this Benjie, you just play on your own side of the street."

Everyone climbed into the Cleaver car and Mr. Cleaver drove home, letting Benjie and Mrs. Bellamy off before he turned into his driveway.

Larry was waiting on the back steps. "Hi, Beav," he said. "I thought up a keen trick—"

"Oh, no, you don't," said Mr. Cleaver as he climbed out of the car. "Now see here, you two boys have caused enough trouble around here with your magic."

"Well, gee, Dad," protested Beaver. "I didn't expect it to turn out that way. We didn't do it on *purpose*."

"I know you didn't, but just the same—" began Mr. Cleaver.

"—we aren't going to have any more magic tricks around here," finished Mrs. Cleaver. "You boys just find something else to amuse yourselves during spring vacation."

"O.K., Mom," answered Beaver and as his mother and father went into the house he sat down beside

Larry and pulled out of his pocket a magazine he had bought in the bus station while he was waiting for the bus to Mayfield. There were a lot of good advertisements in the back that told about things to send away for. Books on how to be a ventriloquist, muscle-developers, things like that.

"It's sure lucky you got to come back before spring vacation was over," remarked Larry.

"Yeah," agreed Beaver. "Only maybe it wasn't luck. Maybe it was magic."

BEAVER PLAYS BALL

Sometimes on report card day Beaver was in no hurry to go home. Sometimes he stopped at Larry Mondello's house as long as he dared and when he did reach home he pretended to have forgotten it was report card day until someone—usually his father, reminded him.

But not today. Today Beaver was in a hurry to go home and show off his report card which was the best one Miss Landers had ever given him. It was so good that even old Judy Hensler who always got

better report cards could not act snippy about it and
that made Beaver happy. Usually whatever Beaver
did, Judy could do better—but not this time.

"Mom! Hey, Mom!" yelled Beaver bursting into
the kitchen.

"Why, what's the matter, Beaver?" asked Mrs.
Cleaver, turning from the kitchen sink.

"Nothing's the matter," answered Beaver, holding
out his report card. "I just got my report card is all."

His mother took it from him. "Well, this is fine,"
she said as she read the card. "B plus . . . B plus . . .
A minus and B."

"And look how good I did in the stuff down at
the bottom," said Beaver eagerly. "Except physical
education. I didn't do so good in that."

Mrs. Cleaver continued to read. "B plus in cour-
tesy . . . B plus in cooperation . . . and A in citizenship."

"Larry Mondello got a C in citizenship," remarked
Beaver.

"That's too bad," said Mrs. Cleaver.

"Yeah, one morning he chewed gum all during
the pledge allegiance," explained Beaver.

"Beaver, I am very proud of you," said Mrs.
Cleaver. "You did very well in all the important
things."

"Gee, thanks, Mom," said Beaver, and then added,
"Do me a favor, will you? Don't tell Dad about my
good marks. Let him read them off the card himself."

Mrs. Cleaver smiled. "All right, Beaver. I'll let him
find out for himself."

Beaver went out to play but he stayed where he

could see his father's car when he came home from work, and when Mr. Cleaver did turn into the driveway Beaver waved and went into the kitchen to wait for him.

"Report card day for the Beaver," announced Mrs. Cleaver when she had kissed her husband. "You're supposed to read it off the card yourself."

"Oh? Good news?" said Mr. Cleaver, taking the card. Beaver watched his father smile and then suddenly he saw the smile fade into a frown. "What's this?" asked Mr. Cleaver. "D in Physical Education?"

"Oh, Ward—" protested Mrs. Cleaver. "He did so well in everything else. Why bring that up?"

"I don't know," said Mr. Cleaver. "It just sort of hit me. Beaver, this is a fine card and I am proud of you. And with all these other good marks, I guess we can excuse a D in physical education."

"Thanks, Dad," said Beaver, but somehow things were not quite the same. He could not help feeling that if his father really had been proud of him he would not have mentioned the D first. He would have left it to the last or perhaps not mentioned it at all.

Then Wally came in through the back door.

"Oh, hi, Wally," said Mr. Cleaver. "How did you make out in the track meet today?"

Wally grinned at his father. "Well, I ran the four-forty in fifty-eight seconds flat."

"Is that good?" asked Mrs. Cleaver.

"Not bad for a freshman," said Mr. Cleaver. "Wally, you ought to make a freshman letter."

"Yeah," said Wally modestly. "I got enough points already."

"Say, Dad, did you notice I got A in citizenship?" asked Beaver, hoping to share his father's approval. "Larry Mondello got C."

"That's fine, Beaver," said Mr. Cleaver. "Say, Wally, when you went to Beaver's school, wasn't the same gym teacher there then?"

"You mean Mr. Grover?" asked Wally. "Sure. He was there. He's a tall guy with a whistle around his neck. He doesn't let you goof off too much, but he's fair."

"Oh, sure," remarked Beaver, feeling dejected. "He's fair all right." He wished Wally would keep out of this. Why couldn't he go to do his homework or go over to Eddie Haskell's house or something?

"Then your D was a fair mark?" Mr. Cleaver asked his younger son.

"Yeah," answered Beaver even more dejectedly. "I guess I was goofing off too much because I'm not much good at tumbling." He wondered why Wally always seemed to be good at things he did poorly. Wally was just naturally good at tumbling and Beaver was not. Beaver's flip-flops were more flop than flip —instead of landing lightly on his feet he usually fell with a thud that knocked a cloud of dust out of the tumbling mats in the gymnasium. Until now he had not minded much. Larry Mondello, who was fat and slow, was not much good at tumbling either. Beaver began to dread his next physical education class. Knowing that his father did not approve was not going to help his tumbling any.

But the next day, Beaver was spared flopping when he should have been flipping because Mr.

Grover ordered, "Line up in front of the screen and we'll have a little batting practice. We're going to get ready for our annual baseball game between the boys and the girls next Monday."

Without much hope Beaver stood in line with the rest of the class. He probably would not be any better at baseball than he was at tumbling, but at least he could not be any worse. He thought of Wally with enough points in three different sports to earn a letter and thought that when he reached high school he probably wouldn't even be good enough to carry water for the football team.

Larry who was first in line picked up the bat with a look of determination. Mr. Grover pitched the ball to him, he swung the bat, hit the ball and grinned with pleasure while the class murmured its surprise and approval. Larry was usually not good at sports. Whitey was next. He swung and missed.

"Boy, are you awful, Whitey," said Judy Hensler and the class giggled.

On the next ball Whitey swung, connected and hit the ball over the heads of the outfielders while the class cheered. He shot Judy a you're-not-so-smart look as he handed Beaver the bat.

Beaver pulled his baseball cap out of his hip pocket and clapped it on his head. Here goes, he thought, without much hope.

"Keep your hands closer together, Beaver," directed Mr. Grover.

Beaver obeyed and waited for the ball. Mr. Grover started to pitch and then stopped. "Stand up to the plate," he said.

Feeling as if he could not do anything right, Beaver stepped closer to the plate and waited with dread for that ball to come whizzing toward him. Mr. Grover wound up and let the ball fly. It seemed to be coming at him so fast that Beaver shut his eyes, swung the best he could and missed. The rest of the boys and girls laughed. Beaver felt embarrassed and ashamed, but he decided that as long as the class was going to laugh anyway, he might as well try to be funny. He twisted his cap around so the visor was in back and pounded the plate with his bat. Obligingly, the boys and girls laughed.

Mr. Grover pitched, Beaver swung a mighty swing that missed just as he knew it would. He shaded his eyes and pretended to look after a ball flying off into the distance and when the class laughed harder this time, a feeling of satisfaction came over him. This was the way to do it. Next he waggled the bat and then held up his hand for Mr. Grover to wait. He removed his cap and used it to brush off the plate.

"Come on, Beaver," said Mr. Grover. "You have only one more strike."

Beaver decided to make the most of it and get a really big laugh. He waved the imaginary infielders out, waggled his bat once more and took his stance. Mr. Grover pitched. Not even caring whether he hit the ball or not, Beaver swung so hard he spun himself around several times while the rest of the class shouted with laughter. With a satisfied grin Beaver handed the bat to the next boy and stepped back into line. That was the way to do it—make everyone laugh. Why should he want to beat the other fellows anyway? They were all his friends.

"Boy, Beaver, were you ever funny!" said Larry with admiration.

"Yes," said Judy, "but what I want to know is, was he funny because he wanted to be funny or was he funny because he is no good?"

Because he was feeling cocky Beaver was able to give Judy a look that left her with nothing to say. It was really easy. He wished he had thought of clowning his way through tumbling so that the class and maybe even Mr. Grover would think he flopped on purpose just to make everyone laugh. He could have said, "Watch how much dust I knock out of the tumbling mat this time."

Beaver even began to look forward to the next day's baseball practice and to think of all the funny things he could do. He could walk up to the plate with the bat balanced on one finger. He could start to bat right-handed, step around the plate and bat left-handed instead. That ought to get a big laugh.

That was the day Wally came home and announced that he was going to be awarded his freshman letter in an assembly at school. It was easy to see how proud he felt and Beaver was proud of him, too. He was glad his brother was good in so many things—now that he had discovered that if he couldn't be good he could be funny.

Beaver did not even care when his father said, "Well, this is fine, Wally. Your first high school letter. I am really proud of you—so proud that I am going to make you a present of the sweater to wear it on."

"Gee, Dad," said Wally. "It costs nineteen dollars."

"That's all right," Mr. Cleaver assured his oldest son. "Any boy who scores in three different sports in his first year in high school deserves a sweater."

"Boy!" exclaimed Wally. "And here I thought I was going to have to save up my allowance."

"And what about you, Beaver?" asked Mr. Cleaver. "How are you coming along in tumbling?"

"Instead of tumbling we had baseball," answered Beaver.

"How'd you make out?" his father wanted to know.

"Swell," said Beaver, remembering the laughter of his classmates. "I had a lot of fun."

"Good boy," said Mr. Cleaver heartily.

Beaver began to look forward even more to his next physical education class which was a pleasant change from the dread he had felt lately. He would walk up to the plate with the bat balanced on the end of his finger—and then he would take a practice swing so hard he would pretend to knock himself down. That really ought to make the class howl.

And the next day Beaver, with his cap on backwards, did walk up to the plate with the bat balanced on the end of his finger. The bat wavered, fell off his finger and hit him lightly on the head as it fell to the ground. Beaver picked it up and started to balance it again.

"All right, Beaver," said Mr. Grover crisply.

Beaver grasped the bat, took his stance and then pretended to see something on the plate. He brushed away the imaginary something and grasped the bat again before he realized that something was wrong. No one laughed.

Beaver tried harder. Mr. Grover wound up and pitched a perfect strike. Beaver swung, missed and twisted himself around like a corkscrew. Still nobody laughed.

"That's all, Beaver," said Mr. Grover.

Not knowing quite what to think, Beaver walked over to the bench and sat down between Whitey and Larry. He grinned hopefully and said, "Hey, Larry, that was pretty funny the way I twisted myself around, huh?"

"Maybe it was funny yesterday," answered Larry, "but it isn't funny today. It's just plain dumb."

"Yeah, Beaver," agreed Whitey. "How are we going to beat the girls next week if you're always kidding around?"

"Aw, anybody can beat girls," said Beaver, still wondering what had gone wrong this afternoon. The class was supposed to laugh, not jump on him. If he was funny yesterday, why wasn't he funny today? Beaver continued to wonder until it was Judy's turn at bat. "You just watch," he said to the other boys. "I bet old Judy is going to be funnier than I was."

Judy flipped her pigtails over her shoulders and grasped the bat. "I'm going to show you how Beaver does it," she announced, crossing her eyes and sticking her tongue out one corner of her mouth. She swung wildly at the ball, missed and stared off into the distance as if she thought she had knocked it clear out of the schoolyard.

The whole class laughed. How do you like that,

thought Beaver crossly, everybody laughed at Judy when they didn't laugh at him.

"That's enough of that, Judy," said Mr. Grover. "Let's get down to business."

Beaver began to smile. Let's see her miss this one a mile, he thought.

Judy set her jaw and waited for the ball. When it came she clouted it so hard it sailed over the heads of the outfielders, over the fence and out of the school grounds and across the street.

Beaver stopped smiling. The class stared after the ball in awed silence as one of the outfielders ran out the gate and across the street after it.

"Boy, is she ever good!" said Whitey, breaking the silence. "I knew she was good, but I didn't know she was *that* good."

"Yeah, Beaver," agreed Larry. "She made you look like a rusty gate."

"Aw, I'll be a lot better when we really play the game," he muttered.

Judy swaggered toward her place on the bench. "How do you like that, Beaver?" she asked in that annoying, snippy way of hers.

"Beaver, what makes you think you'll get to play in the game?" asked Larry. "There are more than nine boys in the class. They can't all be in the game."

"Yeah, Beav," agreed Whitey. "What makes you think you are good enough to play against girls?"

Beaver folded his arms and scowled at the ground. He felt like two cents—no, he didn't even feel that good. To have a girl, and especially that old Judy, show him up in front of the whole class . . . to have

her get the laughs *and* knock the ball over the fence
. . . And then Beaver began to understand. The class
laughed at Judy because they knew she was really
good and they had stopped laughing at him because
they had caught on that he really could not hit the
ball. He was terrible and they knew it. He was so
bad that he might not even get to play in the game
at all, and that was pretty bad, when a fellow didn't
get to play in a game against girls.

Well, he would show Judy and he would show the
class . . . he didn't know how, but Beaver Cleaver
was going to show them.

That afternoon as soon as the school bus dropped
Beaver at his house he hastily made a peanut butter
and baloney sandwich, borrowed Wally's ball and bat
and ran all the way back to school. Except for some
girls playing hopscotch and a couple of little boys
trying to swing all the way across the traveling bars,
he had the school yard to himself. That was the way
he wanted it because he had work to do. This was
Friday and the game was Monday. If he worked hard
all week-end . . .

Beaver stationed himself in front of the screen,
tossed up the ball, swung and missed. He was not
surprised. He simply picked up the ball and started
all over again. He would show his class and everybody else. Doggedly he tossed, swung and most of
the time missed. He did manage to hit the ball often
enough to feel encouraged. Toss, swing, miss. Toss,
swing, swat. He would show everybody he was not
only good enough to play in a game against girls, he
was good enough to hit homeruns.

Beaver worked on and on. For a while he thought he really was improving and then as the shadows on the schoolyard grew longer he missed the ball more and more often. He felt tired and hot and sweaty and then he began to be angry at that ball, that round thing that stubbornly refused to be hit. His swings grew more and more wild. Dusk came and the afternoon grew chilly.

"Hey, Beaver!" It was Wally's voice.

Beaver turned and saw his brother sitting on his bicycle at the curb.

"What do you think you're doing at this time of day?" Wally wanted to know.

'Practicing," answered Beaver and tossed the ball again. He swung and missed.

"Well, cut it out," said Wally. "It is dinnertime and I've been looking all over for you. Come on, I'll ride you home on my bike."

Tired and completely discouraged, Beaver picked up the ball and walked out through the gate. He was never going to be any good. He knew that now. He would never show the class or anybody else.

"Golly, Beaver," said Wally with a smile. "Nothing is as bad as all that. It couldn't be."

"It is, too," said Beaver crossly. "Just because you are good at everything, you don't know what it is to have all the kids think you're no good." He sat on the cross piece of the bicycle and as Wally began to pedal toward home, the street lights came on.

"I didn't used to be any good," said Wally. "All it takes to be good is practice."

"What did you think I was doing?" snapped

Beaver. "I've been practicing and I still can't hit the ball."

"Sure you can't if you think you can't," said Wally.

"I *know* I can't," said Beaver

"Sure you can't," agreed Wally easily. "Not when you're scared of the ball."

Beaver thought this over. He had not realized that he was afraid of the ball, but now that Wally mentioned it, he knew that this was true. That was exactly how he felt when Mr. Grover pitched. It did seem silly, being scared of a ball.

"And you have to remember to keep your eye on the ball," continued Wally as he pumped toward home. "I was watching you. You just throw the ball up and swing any old way without watching what you're supposed to be hitting."

Beaver did not answer. Now that he had stopped swinging the bat he had begun to shiver.

"I tell you what," said Wally. "Tomorrow is Saturday. I'll come over to the school yard and pitch a few balls for you. How would that be?"

"S-swell," answered Beaver through chattering teeth.

Mrs. Cleaver was at the back door looking out into the darkness when the boys rode up the driveway. "Beaver Cleaver!" she exclaimed. "Where on earth have you been? I've been worried to death and dinner has been drying out in the oven!"

"He was just over at the school yard batting a few balls," explained Wally as they went into the house.

"A few!" exclaimed Mrs. Cleaver and then she saw Beaver in the light of the kitchen.

"Why, Beaver, you're shivering all over!" Mrs. Cleaver sounded concerned.

"Getting overheated in the cold like that you could have caught pneumonia." Mrs. Cleaver was both cross and worried. "What a foolish thing to do!"

"Aw, relax, Mom," said Wally. "How do you expect him to get to be a baseball player if he doesn't practice?"

"That's right," agreed Mr. Cleaver. "Beaver, you go upstairs and take a hot bath and get into bed. I'll bring your dinner upstairs on a tray."

Comforted by the knowledge that the men in his family understood, Beaver dragged himself upstairs.

The next morning after breakfast Wally brought out the ball, bat and glove. "Come on, Beav," he said. "Let's go."

Beaver wiggled his shoulders experimentally to see how stiff and sore his muscles were from all the exercise the day before. They were sore all right but not enough to keep him from practicing some more. "Wait till I get my cap," he said to Wally.

"Now Wally," said Mrs. Cleaver, "don't you wear Beaver out."

"Aw, Mom," protested Beaver. "The way you talk you would think I was a little kid."

"Now remember, keep your eye on the ball, and don't try to beat it to death. Just hit it," instructed Wally when the boys reached the school yard. "And don't act scared of the ball."

Beaver wiped his hands on his pants and grasped the bat. He stared at the ball in Wally's hand. You can't scare me, you old ball, he thought ferociously as his eyes followed the motion of Wally's hands. Wally wound up and let go of the ball. Here it came. Beaver's eyes did not waver. He swung the bat. *Smack!*

"Hey, it worked!" he yelled as the ball sailed off over Wally's head.

"Sure it worked," answered Wally over his shoulder as he ran after the ball.

The second time Beaver gave a mighty swing and missed. "How come?" he asked disappointed. "I kept my eye on the ball like you said."

"Golly, Beav," said Wally as he caught the ball Beaver threw back to him. "You can't expect to hit them all. Even big league players don't do that."

"Yeah, I guess so," agreed Beaver, recalling the games he had watched on television.

The boys worked all morning and by lunchtime Beaver was considerably more cheerful. Maybe he wasn't ready for the big league yet, but he was certainly good enough to play a fifth grade ball game against girls including old Judy Hensler. Sure he didn't hit every ball, but what of it? With Wally's coaching he was as good as a lot of the boys in his class. A lot of people were going to be pretty surprised when Monday afternoon came around.

"Well, boys, how did you make out?" asked Mr. Cleaver as the family sat down to lunch.

"O.K., Dad," answered Wally. "He's doing all right for a kid his age. And if we get in some practice this afternoon and after Sunday School tomorrow, he will have the hang of it. I'm going to drop by after school Monday and watch the game."

"Yeah, Dad," said Beaver. "I'm really going to show 'em Monday."

"Wally, you didn't get the Beaver all tired out, did you?" asked Mrs. Cleaver as she poured the milk.

Wally grinned. "I don't know about Beav, but I got pretty tired chasing all those balls he knocked off to the other end of the playground."

But when Monday afternoon came, Beaver soon saw that he was not going to have the opportunity he hoped for, because Mr. Grover, not knowing of his work over the weekend, did not consider him good enough to play in the game. Beaver found himself sitting on the bench watching the other boys play. He squirmed and fidgeted wishing he could get in and show everybody. Helped by Judy's hitting, the girls were soon ahead three to two. Beaver could only cheer the boys on half-heartedly because he felt left out.

Then one of the boys turned his ankle. Beaver looked hopefully at Mr. Grover but the gym teacher chose someone else to replace the boy. Beaver continued to squirm unhappily. He was discouraged. Maybe Mr. Grover was right. In spite of Wally's coaching, he wasn't as good as he thought he was. Still, he would like to be playing when Wally came by to watch the game as he had promised—even though it was a game being won by girls.

And then during the first half of the ninth inning when the girls were at bat and the score was still three to two in their favor, the mother of the boy who was first baseman came and took him out of the game because he had an appointment with the dentist.

Maybe this was his chance. Eagerly Beaver jumped up from the bench. "Me! Me!" he shouted, pointing to himself. "How about me?"

Mr. Grover smiled somewhat ruefully. "All right, Beaver," he agreed. "Suppose you go out in right field."

The boy who was playing right field replaced the first baseman and Beaver ran out to take his place. Right field was the place where he could do the least damage to the game, but at least he was in the game and that was something. Besides, he would be the fourth boy to bat.

The first half of the ninth inning ended with the score still three to two in favor of the girls. Now it was the boys' turn to bat and Judy Hensler was pitching. Beaver could not help wishing it was some other girl. Judy would probably stick her tongue out at him as she pitched and get him all confused. No, she wouldn't either. He was going to keep his eye on the ball not on Judy.

Beaver soon felt a surge of confidence because he could see that Judy was getting tired. Whitey, who was first at bat, got a hit and reached first base. He moved to second when Larry, who followed him at bat, also got a hit. Beaver began to feel excited. Maybe something was going to happen after all.

When it was Gilbert's turn at bat, Judy was even more tired. Beaver watched eagerly as she pitched four balls and could not get one of them over the strike zone. The boys cheered as Gilbert walked to

first base and Whitey and Larry moved on to third
and second.

"What's the matter, Judy?" jeered the boys. "Don't
you know how to pitch?"

Being Judy, she stuck out her tongue, but Beaver
could see she had lost her usual bounce.

Now it was Beaver's turn. He picked up the bat
and looked around the field. It was the ninth inning,
the bases were loaded and *he* had to bat. His courage
began to drain out of him.

Then the other boys began to boo.

Beaver looked miserably at Mr. Grover.

"Beaver, it's up to you," said the teacher. "Think
you can do it?"

Beaver gulped.

"Sure you can!" It was Wally's voice.

"Sure I can, Mr. Grover," answered Beaver. He
wiped his sweating hands on the seat of his pants
and gripped the bat again.

Judy made a face at Beaver, wound up and
pitched. Rattled by the face she made, Beaver forgot
all that Wally had told him, swung as hard as he
could without watching what he was doing and
missed the ball.

"Take it easy," shouted Wally. "Keep your eye on
the ball!"

"No coaching from the sidelines," yelled Judy.

Grimly Beaver kept his eyes on the ball, saw that
the next pitch would be low and did not swing.

"Ball one!" announced Mr. Grover.

The next pitch was also low. Again Beaver did
not swing.

"Ball two," said Mr. Grover.

"Come on, Beaver," yelled the crowd. Beaver tightened his grip on the bat. His heart was banging against his ribs and his mouth felt dry.

"You can do it!" yelled Wally.

Judy was extra careful. A lot depended on this ball. She sent it right over the plate.

Beaver, his eye on the ball, swung the bat, met the ball squarely and sent it down the right field line. He felt stunned by what he had done.

"Run! Run!" yelled the boys while the girls shrieked the way girls do at such times.

Beaver dropped the bat and his feet began to pound. He reached first base, tripped and fell over the bag with his face in the dirt. It did not matter. He got there. He pulled himself to his knees, wiped the dust out of his eyes, looked toward home plate and saw that Whitey had already scored and Larry was puffing into home to score the winning run.

It was over! The boys had won four to three and Beaver found himself a hero. He had a dirty face and a skinned nose but he was a hero just the same. He was surrounded by the boys in his class who were cheering and pounding him on his back. Discovering that he had also skinned his knees, through his jeans, Beaver got stiffly to his feet.

"Boy, Beaver, what a spill you took," said Whitey, but there was admiration in his voice.

"Yeah, too bad you can't see your face," said Larry, still short of breath from his run.

"Beaver bit the dust!" yelled Judy. "And I'll bet he got a mouthful."

Everybody laughed. Beaver grinned. This time the class laughed because they were on his side. And they were on his side, not because he was a clown, but because they knew he was really good. That ought to show old Judy Hensler.

"Maybe he bit the dust, but he won the game," said Mr. Grover who had joined the group. "Congratulations, Beaver."

"Thanks, Mr. Grover," said Beaver modestly. This time he ought to get an A or at least a B plus in physical education. And tonight at dinner he would say casually to his father, we played baseball against the girls today. And his father would say, Oh? How did you make out? And Beaver would say, Oh, I just won the game is all. And Wally would say, That's right, Dad. Mr. Grover said so.

Beaver wiped his face on his sleeve, hitched up his pants and grinned. Wally was no longer the only athlete in the Cleaver family!

BEAVER AND THE SCHOOL SWEATER

The whole Cleaver family was proud the day
Wally wore his high school letterman's sweater home
for the first time. It was easy to see that Wally was
pretty pleased to own that blue sweater with the
yellow M and the yellow stripe around the sleeve.
"Thanks for buying it for me, Dad," he said. "I would
have had to save my allowance a long time to get
nineteen dollars." Other than thanking his father,
Wally did not say much. He just looked happy.

Mr. Cleaver, on the other hand, said a lot. He said
he was proud to have a son who earned enough

47

points in three different sports to win a letter his first year in high school. He said he had been pretty good when he was a boy but he hadn't been that good. Yes sir, he was mighty proud to have a son like Wally and was glad to pay for his sweater. He hoped in a few years to buy a sweater for Beaver, too, now that Beaver was the kind of boy who won baseball games.

Mrs. Cleaver said to think her boy Wally who had been just a little fellow not long ago—it seemed like yesterday—could do a thing like that. She also said she was glad that Mayfield High's colors were blue and yellow because the blue sweater was so becoming to Wally. It made his eyes look even bluer.

Beaver felt the sweater with his fingers. It was a little scratchy and smelled of clean wool and was still so new it had not yet lost the creases in the sleeves. The letter, still spotless, felt luxuriously thick. The sweater made Wally seem older and more important, no longer just an older brother, but an older brother who was somebody special. "Boy, Wally," said Beaver, hoping some of the specialness would rub off on him, "just wait till the kids at school see my brother wearing a letterman's sweater! I guess they are going to be pretty impressed."

"Aw . . ." said Wally modestly.

The next day Beaver lost no time in spreading the news of Wally's sweater. He told Larry and Whitey and Judy, especially Judy, and all the rest of the class and Miss Landers just how good his brother Wally was. And since Beaver had practically won the ball game against the girls singlehanded, although of course it helped to have three fellows on the bases when it was his turn at bat, he couldn't help it if the class thought, Say, maybe Beaver will earn a letter when he is a freshman in high school, too. Not that Beaver bragged or anything like that. He just told the news. He did not have to brag. It did occur to him, however, that he would like to try on Wally's sweater just to see what it felt like.

While Beaver was in school rain began to fall. After school Beaver stopped at Larry's house on the way home and then had to wait until a heavy shower was over before he could leave. When he finally reached his own house he found Wally already studying at his desk in the room the two boys shared.

"Say, Wally," Beaver said. "I told all the kids at school about your sweater."

Wally turned around. "You did? What did they say?"

"They were pretty impressed," said Beaver. "Say uh, Wally, mind if I try your sweater on for just a minute? You know, to sort of see what it feels like to wear a letterman's sweater."

"No, Beav," said Wally. "I mean—no, I don't mind except I . . . uh . . . sort of don't have the sweater right now."

"How come?" asked Beaver.

"It's . . . sort of at school," said Wally and turned back to his studies as if he did not want any further interruptions.

Naturally a fellow wouldn't want to wear a brand-new sweater home in the rain, thought Beaver, but he could roll it up and carry it under his arm or even wrap it up in a copy of the school paper. If Beaver had a letterman's sweater you wouldn't catch him letting it out of his sight.

The next morning it was still raining. Right after breakfast Beaver put on his raincoat, hood and boots and started out the door.

"Why Beaver," said Mrs. Cleaver, "the bus won't be along for another ten minutes."

"I know," agreed Beaver. "This way there will be plenty of time to stand around in the rain."

"But I don't like you standing out there in the wet," protested Mrs. Cleaver.

"Gee, Mom, what's the good of having rain if you can't stand around in it?" asked Beaver.

"That's right," agreed Mr. Cleaver. "Standing in the rain is a boy's right."

Then Wally got up from the table and picked up his school books.

"Wally, where's your raincoat?" asked Mrs. Cleaver. "You can't go out in the rain in slacks and a sport shirt."

"I don't need it," answered Wally. "I'm running to school."

"You'll get soaking wet," pointed out Mrs. Cleaver who was inclined to be fussy about things like raincoats and wet feet.

"No, I won't," said Wally. "I'll run under trees and awnings and stuff. I won't get wet at all."

"I think you better wear a sweater, Wally." Mr. Cleaver meant what he said.

Beaver thought then that there was something peculiar about the way Wally was acting because he said, "Gee, Dad, I don't have a sweater that fits me."

"Of course you do," answered his father. "You have your letterman's sweater."

"Oh, well, that's . . . uh . . . sort of at school," Wally answered with great reluctance.

"Sort of at school?" questioned Mrs. Cleaver. "Wally, you haven't lost it, have you?"

"No . . . I haven't lost it," answered Wally.

"That sweater cost nineteen dollars. You bring it home this evening," ordered Mr. Cleaver.

There is something funny going on, thought Beaver as he went out to stand in the rain to wait for the school bus. Wally wasn't acting . . . well, like Wally. And to leave that sweater at school the second day he had it—it didn't make sense.

When Beaver climbed aboard the bus, Whitey said the very first thing, "Hey, Beaver, how come I saw your brother coming home from school yesterday and he wasn't wearing a letterman's sweater like you said?"

"Search me," answered Beaver, settling into a seat.

"Hey, look!" exclaimed Larry. "There's Wally coming out of the house now and he's wearing a reversible jacket."

The class looked. Beaver slid unhappily down in his seat.

"Yeah, Beaver," said Whitey. "If Wally has a sweater how come he isn't wearing it?"

"Maybe he didn't want to get it wet," suggested Beaver.

The boys and girls jeerd at this. "I'll bet he doesn't have a sweater," scoffed Gilbert. "Any fellow with a new letterman's sweater wears it."

"I'll bet you just made it up," said Judy. "Just because you accidentally happened to bat one ball you think your whole family is a bunch of athletes."

"I do not!" answered Beaver hotly. "And he *does* have a letterman's sweater."

"Quiet down, you kids!" yelled the bus driver. "How do you expect me to drive this bus with you making such a racket?"

That afternoon Beaver waited for Wally to come home from school. When he finally arrived he was still wearing his reversible jacket and there was no sign of his sweater. "Hey, Wally—" Beaver began but Wally cut him short.

"I've got a lot of studying to do," Wally said and went upstairs without even stopping to make a sandwich.

Still hoping Wally might say something about his sweater, Beaver followed, and when Wally really did settle down at his desk and begin to study, Beaver flopped down on the bed and began to read comic books. Probably half his class had seen Wally on the way home from school. And that half would tell the other half that Wally was not wearing a letterman's sweater and tomorrow the whole class would tell Beaver about it.

Before long the doorbell rang. Downstairs Beaver heard his mother telling Wally's friend Eddie Haskell to go on up to the boys' room.

"Did you get it, Wally?" asked Eddie as he came into the room.

"No," answered Wally glumly.

Eddie laughed.

"Get what?" asked Beaver, looking up from his comic book.

"Aw . . . never mind," muttered Wally.

"Didn't you ask her?" Eddie wanted to know.

"Sure I asked her." Wally looked thoroughly unhappy.

"Well, come on," said Eddie impatiently. "What did she say?"

Wally glanced at Beaver. "Aw . . ." he muttered uncomfortably.

"What are you fellows talking about anyway?" demanded Beaver who had not been able to make sense out of the conversation.

"Wally's letterman's sweater," answered Eddie.

"What has a girl got to do with it?" asked Beaver.

"Plenty," answered Eddie with a laugh. "Pa-lenty."

"Oh, all right," said Wally crossly. "Yesterday when it was raining so hard when school was out this girl—"

"—Frances Hobbs," prompted Eddie.

Beaver had never heard Wally mention a girl named Frances Hobbs although he had mentiened Mary Ellen Rogers a couple of times.

"This Frances Hobbs just happened to be standing on the steps and she didn't have any sweater or coat or anything," continued Wally. "She said she was cold and she was giggling and shivering and stuff and . . . well, I let her take my sweater to wear home. That's all. So now you know."

Beaver was shocked. Wally let a *girl* wear his brand new letterman's sweater home. Boy! He certainly hoped the kids at school didn't find this out. And his father—what would he say about it? Of course, he could see why any girl would want to wear a sweater that belonged to a good-looking boy like Wally, but for Wally to *let* her . . .

"Go on," said Eddie eagerly. "What happened when you asked her to give it back."

Wally looked disgusted. "Well . . . she . . . I went up to her and she said the rain made my hair curly and I said we used to have a dog that got curly when it rained—"

Eddie interrupted with a shout of laughter.

Wally ignored him. "And I said if she was finished using my sweater could I have it back and she said sure. She said she would bring it to school the first thing tomorrow."

"But she was wearing it today," said Eddie. "I saw her."

Wally looked uncomfortable. "Well . . . she said it was still raining and I wouldn't want her to get all . . . uh . . . soakie, would I? So what could I say?"

"*Soakie!*" Eddie fell over on the bed laughing. "Boy I can hear her say it." Eddie fluttered his eyelashes and spoke in a squeaky voice, " 'Wally, you wouldn't want me to get all soakie, would you?' "

"Oh, shut up!" said Wally and threw a book at Eddie.

"But Wally," said Beaver when Eddie had left. "This is Friday. You won't get your sweater back till Monday. What are you going to tell Dad?" He did not add that in the meantime practically everybody in Mayfield would see Wally without his sweater and Beaver would have a lot of explaining to do at school on Monday. The worst of it was he couldn't tell them that a *girl* had Wally's sweater. That would be worse than Wally's not having a sweater at all.

"What do you think I've been worrying about?" asked Wally. "Dad's going to blow his top."

"Wally," said Beaver thoughtfully. "It is your sweater. Maybe Dad won't blow his top."

"Look, Beaver," said Wally, turning around from his desk. "When your parents give you something worth nineteen dollars, it may be yours but they have a lot to say about it."

Beaver thought some more. "Wally, why didn't you sock her?"

"Aw, don't be silly, Beaver," answered Wally. "A fellow can't go around socking girls."

"I socked Judy Hensler once," said Beaver.

"That's different. You're just a kid," Wally explained. "At my age it is different. All of a sudden a fellow has to start being polite."

Beaver continued to think. "When I was little, Lumpy Rutherford took my scooter and Dad went over and took it right out of Mr. Rutherford's garage. Why don't you ask Dad to get your sweater back for you?"

Wally sighed. "Beaver, you just don't understand. This is something else that doesn't work that way when you get to be my age. You have to fight your own battles."

Beaver, who had always wished he could catch up with Wally, began to see that there were some disadvantages to growing up. To have to fight your own battles and at the same time not be able to sock a girl—golly!

The boys did not have long to wait for Mr. Cleaver's reaction. When he came home from work he came upstairs and looked into their room. "Well, Wally, did you remember to bring your sweater home?" he asked as Mrs. Cleaver joined him in the doorway.

When Wally hesitated, Beaver blurted, "A *girl* is wearing it." The way Wally scowled at him made him instantly sorry he had spoken.

"A girl!" Mrs. Cleaver sounded shocked. "Why, Wally, you're just a baby!"

"No, he isn't," said Mr. Cleaver. "He is a freshman in high school. We have to expect him to take an interest in girls sometime."

"Wally," said Mrs. Cleaver reproachfully. "I think you might have told us there was a girl you liked."

"Aw, Mom . . ." Wally squirmed in his chair. "You've got it all wrong." As briefly as he could he explained what had happened to his sweater. Beaver noticed he skipped the part about the rain making his hair curly and Frances saying she didn't want to get all soakie.

"Well, all I can say," said Mr. Cleaver when Wally had finished, "all I can say is you better have that sweater back by Monday or else."

Beaver sat up and looked interested. "Or else what, Dad?"

Mr. Cleaver smiled ruefully. "Well, right off the bat I can't think of an 'or else,'" he admitted, "but if Wally doesn't produce that sweater there certainly will be an 'or else.'"

Beaver felt sorry for his brother. It must be pretty

hard to have a brand new letterman's sweater and not get to wear it. He felt almost as sorry for himself. He knew what the riders of the school bus were going to say Monday morning and he also knew that he would never, never admit that a girl, a girl Wally didn't even *like,* had taken Wally's sweater away from him so easily. Sorry as he was, Beaver was also disappointed in Wally. A fellow who was good enough to win a freshman letter should be able to hang onto the sweater.

Saturday afternoon Larry Mondello came over to see Beaver. "How about letting me see Wally's sweater?" he asked. "If he really has one."

"I don't know where Wally is right now," answered Beaver truthfully. "How about letting me treat you to a soda at the drugstore? I got my allowance today." Beaver knew that a soda would make Larry forget about the sweater for the time being at least. He was right.

"Oh boy, a whole soda?" asked Larry, "and not just an extra straw in your soda?"

"Sure. A whole soda," said Beaver generously. "Come on, let's go."

When they reached the drugstore the two boys climbed on stools at the counter and after changing their minds several times, Beaver decided on a chocolate soda and Larry on a pineapple soda. When they were served Larry began to eat the ice cream with a spoon. Beaver felt this was cheating. The entire soda should be drunk through a straw no matter how long it took the ice cream to melt.

While the boys, each in his own way, were con-

suming their sodas, three high school girls came into
the drugstore and sat down in a booth directly behind the boys. By stretching his neck Beaver could
see them reflected in the mirror behind the soda
fountain. One of the girls, the prettiest one, was
wearing a freshman letterman's sweater. It was a
new sweater because it still had the creases in the
sleeves. Beaver stopped sucking the straw and stared
at the girl because he had a feeling this must be
Frances Hobbs.

Larry made a slurping noise with his straw. He
lifted it from his glass, held it up and sucked on the
end that had been in the soda. "Piece of pineapple
got stuck in it," he explained as he put the straw
back in his soda.

Beaver ignored Larry. He was trying to hear what
the girls were saying.

The girl in the sweater was speaking. "He's been
trying to get a date with me for two weeks," she
was saying. "He just follows me everywhere."

"I didn't think Wally Cleaver followed any girls,"
said one of her friends.

"Hey, Beav!" exclaimed Larry. "They're talking
about—"

Beaver kicked Larry under the counter. "Shut up,"
he whispered.

The girl in the sweater continued, "Well, he
doesn't, but he told me, 'Frances you're not just any
girl.' Well, come on and let's have our cokes. I had
better be getting home. Wally might phone me. The
poor dear is terribly jealous. He just begged me to
wear his sweater. I finally had to say yes."

It was all Beaver could do to keep from swinging around on his stool and yelling, "He did not!"

"Hey, Beav, did you hear that?" whispered Larry.

"Come on," said Beaver, sliding off his stool. "Let's get out of here."

"Hey, wait a minute," protested Larry. "I haven't finished my soda."

"Well, hurry up," ordered Beaver while Larry sucked at the straw as hard as he could.

While he waited Beaver glared at Frances Hobbs who was completely unaware of him. He wanted to walk right over and punch her in the nose. Suddenly he began to understand what Wally was up against. A boy could not punch a girl Frances' age in the nose. Why, she was even worse than old Judy Hensler who at least did not go around flapping her eyelashes. Poor Wally.

Larry finally made the loud noise that meant he had sucked the last of his soda out of his glass. Then he licked the outside of the straw and was finished. "Did you hear that girl?" he asked as they left the drugstore. "She said Wally begged her to wear his sweater."

"I told you he had a sweater." Beaver tried to sound triumphant, but under the circumstances he could not manage it.

"Yeah, but to let a *girl* wear it—" Larry implied that Wally might as well not have a sweater at all if he was going to waste it on a girl.

"Well, she was lying, that's what she was doing," said Beaver hotly.

"Then how come she was wearing the sweater?" asked Larry.

Beaver could not answer him. He could scarcely tell Larry what had happened. What would Larry think of a brother who let a girl borrow his sweater and then couldn't get it back? And then a doubt crept into Beaver's mind. Perhaps it was Wally who had not been telling the truth. Perhaps he really did like Frances and did not want his family to know about it, especially since he liked her enough to let her wear a nineteen-dollar sweater the very first day he got it. After all, his father had told him to bring the sweater back and he had not done so. Beaver did not know what to think.

"You know, Beaver," said Larry, "that girl was kind of pretty."

"Yeah," agreed Beaver. "Maybe that's the whole trouble."

Later that afternoon Beaver found his brother alone in their room. "Me and Larry had a soda at the drugstore this afternoon," he began casually. "Guess who we saw?"

"Whitey?" Wally did not sound much interested.

"Nope." Beaver sprung his surprise. "Frances Hobbs."

"No kidding." Wally sounded disgusted. That was a hopeful sign.

"She has real flappy eyelashes," remarked Beaver, hoping to draw Wally out.

"Yeah." Wally agreed so he must have noticed her eyelashes, too. Suddenly he swung around on his chair and faced Beaver. "How come you knew

Frances Hobbs when you saw her?" he demanded. "She doesn't live around here."

"Because she was wearing a letterman's sweater and she was talking about Wally Cleaver," answered Beaver.

Wally looked suspicious. "What did she say?"

"Oh, stuff like how you follow her everywhere and—" Beaver was interrupted.

"You're making that up," accused Wally.

"Honest, I'm not," said Beaver. "She said worse stuff than that. She said you begged her to wear your sweater."

"Boy!" exclaimed Wally.

"—and how you were terribly jealous—" Beaver continued.

Wally interrupted again. "Gee *whiz!*"

"—and how she finally had to say yes," finished Beaver.

Wally stood up. "Boy, oh, boy! Have I ever been taken! So she didn't want to get all soakie! Boy!"

Beaver had never seen his good-natured brother so angry.

Wally grabbed his jacket from the bedpost.

"Where you going, Wally?" asked Beaver.

"Over to that creepy Frances' house to get my sweater," answered Wally and left the bedroom, slamming the door behind him.

Beaver grabbed his own jacket. "Hey, Wally, wait for me!" he yelled as he opened the door and ran down the stairs.

"What's going on here?" demanded Mr. Cleaver as Beaver clattered down the stairs.

"Boy, Dad—this is going to be good," answered Beaver and ran out the front door and down the street after Wally. "Wally! Hey, Wally! Wait for me!"

Wally who had sprinted down the street as if he were running in a track meet, stopped and waited for Beaver. "Boy!" he was muttering when Beaver reached him. "*Boy!*"

When the boys reached Frances' house, Wally punched the doorbell with his thumb and stood glowering at the door. Beaver glowered, too. That Frances had caused them both plenty of trouble.

Frances opened the door. "Why, Wally Cleaver!" she exclaimed, all smiles and flapping eyelashes.

"Hello, Frances," said Wally coldly.

"Why Wally, this must be your cute little brother," said Frances.

Beaver hoped he looked menacing, like a villain on television. "Yeah," he answered. "I'm his cute little brother."

"Oh, Wally!" squealed Frances. "He's *darling!*"

I am not, thought Beaver, still scowling. Darling! How creepy could Frances get, anyway?

"Frances—" began Wally.

The girl interrupted. "Helen is here and we're making fudge. Won't you boys come in and have some?"

"No, thank you," answered Wally. "I want my sweater."

"Oh," said Frances. "I'm going to bring it to school Monday, Wally." Those eyelashes again.

"No," said Wally. "Would you please go get it right now?"

"Well . . . all right, Wally . . ." Frances smiled prettily. "Won't you come in?"

"I'll wait here." Wally remained stern.

When Frances had gone to get the sweater, Beaver whispered, "After you get the sweater, maybe we could have some fudge."

"No," said Wally flatly. "Frances is the kind of girl that if we ate her fudge I never would get my sweater back."

The boys waited. "Maybe she's gone to get her mother to chase us off," suggested Beaver.

"I'm not leaving until I get my sweater." Beaver had never seen Wally act so determined.

Finally after the boys had a long wait, Frances returned to the door with Wally's sweater. "Here it is, Wally." She smiled prettily as if she were doing him a big favor to let him have his own sweater.

"Thank you." Wally took the sweater. "And another thing—you just watch what you're saying around in drugstores about me."

"Why, Wally, whatever do you mean?" asked Frances innocently.

"Just watch it, that's all," said Wally and turned to leave.

"I guess we really told her, didn't we, Wally?" said Beaver as they walked down the steps. He wished he could learn to talk that way to that old Judy Hensler. Maybe he could when she reached the eyelash flapping stage. Now she would just stick out her tongue at anything he said.

"Sure," agreed Wally pulling off his jacket and putting on the sweater. "We told her all right."

Beaver sniffed. "You know something, Wally? You smell kind of girly."

"That's perfume or some kind of junk," answered Wally. "I'll hang the sweater in my gym locker with my sneakers a couple of days. That ought to kill it."

Beaver looked admiringly at his older brother. He was a brother to be proud of. He had not only earned the right to wear a letterman's sweater, he could walk right up to a girl and demand that she give it back. He didn't even have to threaten to punch her in the nose. "Say, Wally—" Beaver began and hesitated.

"What?" asked Wally.

"Well, I was wondering if on Monday morning about the time the school bus comes by for me, you could sort of walk out of the house in your letterman's sweater and . . ." Beaver's voice trailed off. He was a little embarrassed to make such a request of Wally.

Wally grinned. "—and let all the kids see I really have a sweater?" he finished for Beaver.

"Yes," answered Beaver. "How did you guess?"

"Well—" Now it was Wally's turn to look embarrassed. "I had been thinking that I would sort of like to wear my sweater and walk past the school I used to go to . . ."

"So everybody could see how good you are?" finished Beaver.

"Well . . . yes, I guess you could put it that way," admitted Wally. "But it would be better if I just

happen to walk out of the house when the school
bus stops. That way it wouldn't look as if I'm trying
to show off."

"Swell," said Beaver happily. He could hardly
wait until Monday morning when he would get to
show off Wally not showing off!

WALLY'S HAIRCOMB

One Saturday afternoon Beaver and Larry Mondello found themselves with nothing to do. One boy would think of something and the others would find fault with the idea. Larry suggested they go fishing. Beaver said their mothers would not let them. Beaver suggested they go over to the park and try chinning themselves ten times without stopping. Larry said he did not feel like it and besides he weighed too much. Beaver suggested they send away for a book on how to be a ventriloquist. Larry said it would take too long for the book to come.

67

So it went as the boys lay sprawled on Beaver's bed in the room he shared with his brother Wally. They were looking through the magazine Beaver had bought in the bus station the day he returned from Aunt Martha's house. There were so many interesting advertisements in the back of the magazine that they were sure to come across some kind of an idea.

"Here is something, Larry," said Beaver, pointing to an advertisement. "See, it says 'Earn money in your spare time.' Wouldn't you like to start earning money in your spare time?"

Wally, who was in the bathroom that opened off the bedroom spoke up. "Aw, that's kid stuff." Wally, who had curly hair, spent a lot of time in the bathroom trying to slick his hair down, but it seemed as if the more he slicked, the more his hair curled. Wally had quite a collection of creams, tonics, lotions and oils, none of them very helpful.

Larry read the advertisement carefully. "It says you can earn seven hundred dollars a month. That's not kid stuff."

"Yeah, but what do you have to do?" asked Wally.

"Just raise chinchillas is all," said Beaver.

"Is all!" scoffed Wally. "What do you know about raising chinchillas?"

"Nothing," admitted Beaver, "but I bet we could learn. Gee, Wally—it says here they are 'clean, friendly little animals' and here is a man in Des Moines who made ten thousand dollars in one year."

"I'll bet," said Wally.

"Aw, you just slick your hair down and keep out of this," said Beaver good-naturedly. He wanted to think that it was possible to earn ten thousand dollars in one year raising chinchillas, and besides, every time Wally tried to slick his hair down, Beaver felt pleasantly superior. His own hair was straight and usually fell over his forehead, but on special occasions—Sunday School, visits to Aunt Martha, birthday parties given by girls—when his mother wanted him to smooth his hair back, all he had to do was comb a little water through it.

"You keep quiet about my hair," said Wally.

"O.K." Beaver pointed to the advertisement. "See . . . ten thousand dollars. It's even signed by the man, Mr. J. T."

"Ten thousand dollars for raising clean friendly little animals," Larry studied the advertisement. "I'll bet chinchillas are something like hamsters. Hamsters are clean, friendly little animals."

"Yeah," agreed Beaver.

"We could have all the ice cream sodas we wanted . . ." began Larry dreamily.

"Larry, don't you ever think about anything besides eating?" asked Wally.

"Sure I do," said Larry. "We could see all the movies we wanted . . ."

"Beaver, how do you know this Mr. J. T. is a real person?" asked Wally, coming out of the bathroom.

"Because here's his picture and he's got a real face." Beaver handed Wally the magazine.

"Aw . . ." Wally looked at the advertisement and threw the magazine down in disgust.

"Boy, you've sure got your hair gooped up this time," Beaver told his brother. "You know what Mom will say about getting greasy stuff all over the pillow case."

"I'll put a towel on the pillow," said Wally and went back into the bathroom.

"Maybe instead of ice cream sodas we could start eating banana splits," day-dreamed Larry. "We could afford it with ten thousand dollars a year to throw around."

"Five thousand a piece," Beaver reminded him.

Wally stuck his head out of the bathroom again. "If you had five thousand dollars a year Dad would make you save most of it."

"You mean if he had that much money his dad could still tell him what to do?" asked Larry.

"Sure he could," said Wally.

Larry seemed disappointed to learn this. "Yeah, I guess you're right. My dad would probably start charging me board and room. Anyway, where could we keep chinchillas?"

Beaver sat up excited. "We could build cages for them and keep them in the garage and pretty soon they would put our pictures in the magazines."

"Yeah!" Larry was enthusiastic. "And wouldn't that be something to show the kids at school."

"We can get started building the cages right now and have them ready when the chinchillas come. Wally, don't you want to help?" asked Beaver. Wally had taken a course in shop at school and was better at building things than either Beaver or Larry.

"Nope," said Wally. "You build your own cages."

"Don't you want to come in on the chinchillas business?" asked Beaver.

Wally grinned. "I got better things to do than make ten thousand dollars a year."

"O.K., but don't come around pestering me when I am rich and you need a pair of track shoes or something," said Beaver. "Larry and I can go build our own chinchilla cages."

Beaver stuck his magazine in his hip pocket and the two boys went out to the garage which that day was empty of the car because it was Mr. Cleaver's turn to drive his neighbor, Mr. Rutherford, to work. They found tools, some old boards, a roll of chicken wire that Mr. Cleaver had once put around the edge of a new lawn to protect it from dogs until the grass was established.

Larry grabbed a board and a saw and announced, "I'm good at sawing."

"Now wait a minute," cautioned Beaver. "We've got to plan before we start sawing. How big is a chinchilla?"

How big was a chinchilla? Neither boy knew. "About as big as a hamster?" suggested Larry.

"I guess maybe so." It sounded logical to Beaver. "They can't be too big or people couldn't raise them at home."

The boys proceeded on the assumption that chinchillas were hamster-sized animals and went to work. They measured and marked the lumber. They cut wire with a pair of wire-cutters. They sawed. None of this was easy because they did not have a workbench or a sawhorse. Assembling the cages was dif-

ficult, too, the boys soon discovered. They thought
they had measured carefully but somehow none of
the pieces seemed to fit together as they had planned.

Larry, who was on his knees trying to nail two
boards together on the cement floor, asked, "Do
you think your father is going to like our building
stuff in his garage?"

"He always says boys need stuff to do at home so
as to keep them off the streets," answered Beaver.

"I think my folks would rather I played on the
streets so I wouldn't mess up the house." Larry
brought the hammer down on his thumb, dropped
the hammer and began to suck his thumb.

"Yow!" said Beaver who was sitting on the floor
snipping away at the roll of chicken wire with the
wire-cutters. "I have scratched myself about fifty
million times with this stuff." He looked around at
the squares of chicken wire scattered on the floor.
"And I've got about fifty million more of these
squares to cut. Larry, do you think we have to be
in such a hurry to get these cages built? It will take
a while for the chinchillas to get here."

"Maybe you're right," agreed Larry. "I've pounded
my thumb about sixty trillion times already."

Just then Wally's friend, Eddie Haskell came up
the driveway. He was combing his curly blond
hair as he walked. "Boy, what a mess!" he remarked,
looking around the garage.

"We're building chinchilla cages," said Beaver.

"Chinchilla cages! Where are you going to get any
chinchillas?" asked Eddie.

"Send away for them," answered Beaver.

"No kidding?" Eddie looked surprised. "Where are you going to get that kind of money?"

"What kind of money?" asked Beaver.

"Chinchillas cost two or three hundred dollars apiece," said Eddie.

Larry dropped the hammer again. "They *do?*"

"Sure," said Eddie. "They make rich ladies' coats out of them and rich ladies aren't going to pay a lot of money for a coat if the animals don't cost a lot of money, are they?"

"You mean you got to kill the chinchillas?" Beaver did not like the idea at all.

"You didn't think people raised them just to pet, did you?" There was something annoying about Eddie's grin.

"Well, no, but—" Beaver did not know what to say.

"I bet you fellows have been reading one of those ads in the back of some magazine that says, 'Earn money in your spare time.'" Eddie began to laugh.

Beaver suddenly felt foolish. "Well, don't stand there laughing," he said crossly.

"I can't help it," said Eddie, laughing harder. "To think you two would fall for something like that."

Then Wally walked into the garage and the chinchillas were forgotten. Beaver and Larry and Eddie were startled into silence. They stood and stared at Wally's hair. Gone were the curls. Instead his hair was flattened on top, combed up on the sides into a sort of roll and the back was combed into crossed duck tails.

Wally was obviously pleased with himself. "What's

the matter? Can't a fellow change the way he wears his hair without everybody staring?" he asked.

Eddie was the first to regain his speech. "Hey, do you look sharp!" He walked around Wally to admire his hair.

"Yeah." At first Beaver had not been sure, but if Eddie said Wally looked sharp, Wally looked sharp. Eddie knew about things like clothes and hair for high school boys. Mr. Cleaver said Eddie was something of a dude, but Beaver and Wally considered him an authority on fashion.

"Is that looking sharp?" asked Larry. "I thought he looked fun—"

"Of course he looks sharp," interrupted Beaver. That dumb Larry!

"How did you do it?" asked Eddie.

"A new kind of hair goo," answered Wally. "The stuff fellows use on crew cuts. I tried it and it works."

Eddie ran his hand over his own hair. "No kidding? Do you think it would work on me?"

"Sure," said Wally. "Want to try some?"

"Could I?" asked Eddie. "And then let's go over to Mary Ellen Rogers' house. She's expecting us."

"Boy, oh, boy!" exclaimed Wally. "What are we waiting for?"

Beaver and Larry were left with the pieces of their chinchilla cages in which they now had lost interest. Two or three hundred dollars apiece for one little chinchilla! Golly!

Larry sat down on a box. "Honest, did you think Wally looked sharp?" he asked.

"Sure he does." Beaver was loyal to his brother,

and after the first surprised moment, he agreed with Eddie.

"I don't know." Larry was still not convinced. "I thought maybe he looked funny."

"Aw, just because you always need a haircut . . ." Beaver would not admit it, but he, too, had some doubts about Wally's hair, not because he did not admire it himself, but because he wondered what his father was going to say.

"I guess Wally sort of likes Mary Ellen Rogers, doesn't he?" ventured Larry.

"I guess so." Beaver kicked at the roll of chicken wire. "Anyway he says she's a good kid and he goes over there every chance he gets."

"I wish there was some fellow that liked my sister," said Larry. "Then maybe she would get married and move away."

"Let's forget about chinchillas." Beaver pulled the magazine out of his pocket and looked at it in disgust. "Let's go look at an old movie on T.V."

Larry glanced around the littered garage. "I just remembered I was supposed to come home early."

On the way into the house Beaver dropped his magazine into the incinerator. He was having a good time in front of the television set laughing at the funny clothes people wore in old movies when he heard his father come home.

"June," called Mr. Cleaver when he entered the back door. "Have you seen the garage?"

"Can't you find it dear?" answered Mrs. Cleaver. "The last time I looked it was right at the end of the driveway."

Beaver slid down in his chair.

"I'm not being funny," said Mr. Cleaver and came into the living room. "Beaver, do you know anything about the mess in the garage?"

"I guess you are talking about the chinchilla cages Larry and I were building until we changed our minds about raising chinchillas," said Beaver. "You always said boys needed stuff to do at home to keep them off the streets."

"Now look here." Mr. Cleaver was stern. "How would you feel if you left the house in the morning and went to your job and worked hard all day trying to make a living and then drove home and opened the garage door and found you couldn't get your car in?"

"Gee, Dad, I don't know." Beaver was a little frightened by his father's outburst. "I'm only in the fifth grade."

This made Mr. Cleaver laugh. "Well, I have a good idea for keeping you off the streets."

"What?" asked Beaver suspiciously.

His father confirmed his suspicion. "Clean up the garage."

And then Wally came whistling up the front walk on his way home from Mary Ellen Rogers' house. He opened the front door and walked in. "Hi, Dad."

Beaver waited for his father to say something.

"Uh . . . hi, Wally," said Mr. Cleaver.

Wally seemed to be waiting for something. "Uh . . . well . . . I guess I better get washed for dinner." He went on upstairs.

"Ward!" exclaimed Mrs. Cleaver when Wally was out of earshot. "Did you see Wally's hair?"

"I saw it all right," admitted Mr. Cleaver. "Nobody could miss it."

"Aren't you going to yell at him, Dad?" asked Beaver.

"It looks like an oil mop," said Mrs. Cleaver. "We can't have him going around looking like that. He looks like a freak."

Mr. Cleaver remained calm. "It's just a fad. He'll probably be combing his hair some other way tomorrow, but I'll drop a hint at dinner. I'm sure Wally will get the idea."

"You'd better," said Mrs. Cleaver. "I can't understand what got into Wally, but I do know something has to be done about it right away. The idea of a good looking boy like Wally going around like that!"

When the family was seated at the dinner table Mr. Cleaver smiled at his oldest son. "Well, Wally, don't your mother and I detect a slight difference in the way you're combing your hair?"

"Gee, Dad, I didn't think you'd notice." Beaver could see that Wally was pleased that his father had noticed. "Lots of the fellows are wearing their hair this way. It's called a Jellyroll."

Mr. Cleaver cleared his throat. "You know, Wally, it's funny—lots of boys will follow every fad that comes along, but there are always a few who have enough individuality to go their own way. You know what I mean, Wally?"

"Sure, Dad," agreed Wally. "At school we call them squares."

Beaver saw his mother and father exchange a glance. Mr. Cleaver's look said, This is going to be harder than I thought. Mrs. Cleaver's look said, For heaven's sake, *do* something. Mr. Cleaver looked thoughtful.

Beaver waited to see what his father would do next. When dessert was served, Mr. Cleaver said, "Wally, aren't they having tryouts for the swimming team this week?"

"That's right, Dad," said Wally. "I thought I would go out for it."

Mr. Cleaver smiled at Wally. "That's fine. But I was just thinking—the way you have your hair, won't it be kind of a handicap?"

"How?" asked Wally.

"You know—it's liable to fall down in your eyes and you might bump smack into the end of the pool." Mr. Cleaver leaned back in his chair with a this-ought-to-do-it look on his face.

"Gee, I never thought of that," said Wally not even noticing the look of relief that crossed his mother's face.

That evening when the boys were getting ready for bed, Wally spent a lot of time in the bathroom combing his hair while Beaver watched through the door. "Gee whiz, when you lie down won't your hair bend?" asked Beaver. "Or do you sleep sitting up?"

"No, I think it's guaranteed not to bend." Wally stopped combing to admire the effect in the mirror. "It's supposed to dry out and get hard."

Beaver was fascinated. "You mean like cement?"

"Something like cement."

Beaver wished he was old enough to have cement hair.

Sunday morning Wally came down to breakfast with his hair combed even higher. Beaver expected his father to tell Wally he could not wear his hair to Sunday School that way, but he said nothing. Beaver heard his mother whispering to his father about something and heard his father answer, "Now, relax, dear."

By the time Sunday School was over Beaver wished even more that he was old enough to have cement hair because Wally was gathering so much attention. Of course, all the grownups they met seemed to be trying not to smile and all the boys and girls Beaver's age laughed and pointed, but they didn't count. It was Wally's friends who were admiring and it was the high school crowd that counted. After Sunday School Wally hung around a while hoping for a chance to walk home with Mary Ellen Rogers, but when she went off with a group of girls, he walked home with Beaver.

That day things were pretty tense around the Cleaver household. Every time Wally was out of hearing, Mrs. Cleaver would say, "Ward, *please* tell Wally to stop combing his hair that awful way. He looks like a tango dancer." And Mr. Cleaver would answer, "Now June, if we just wait a while Wally's own good sense will take over."

Beaver was pretty sure Wally did not have the kind of good sense his father meant.

"But his beautiful curls," Mrs. Cleaver whispered.

"Dear, no boy Wally's age wants beautiful curls," was Mr. Cleaver's answer.

"Eddie Haskell does," said Beaver. "He's always combing his."

And then Eddie came over to see Wally. His curls were gone, too, and his hair was flattened on top and combed up at the sides exactly like Wally's. "Wally, you are right!" he said enthusiastically. "The stuff works."

Mrs. Cleaver gave her husband a desperate, now-see-what-happened look which he returned with a let's-keep-calm look. Then he said to Beaver. "Remember. The garage?"

"Oh, yeah, Dad, the garage." At least cleaning the garage was something to do. Beaver went to the telephone and invited Larry to come over to play. He dropped a hint that Mrs. Cleaver might bake some cookies after a while and so Larry came.

"Come on, let's clean up the garage," said Beaver and when Larry looked as if he might remember he had to go home, he added, "You wanted to get rich raising chinchillas just as much as I did."

Because it is never as much fun to clean up a mess as it is to make one, the boys went to work without much enthusiasm. They picked up nails, rolled chicken wire and stacked boards. Then they sat down to rest. "Did your dad make Wally wash the goop out of his hair?" asked Larry.

"No," answered Beaver. "He's waiting for Wally's good sense to take over. Come on, let's knock apart those cages we built."

"Aw, what's the hurry," protested Larry. "If we

finish we'll be right where we started—nothing to do again."

"Yeah, I suppose so." Nevertheless Beaver picked up a hammer and went to work. The work was not finished by noon so Mrs. Cleaver invited Larry to stay for lunch.

When Wally appeared Beaver saw that his good sense still had not taken over.

"You know, Dad," said Wally, as he pulled out his chair and sat down at the table, "I've been thinking it over and you're right about the swimming team. My hair would get in the way when I swam."

Mrs. Cleaver's face relaxed into a smile and Mr. Cleaver grinned and said, "Good!"

"Yeah," said Wally, "I would have to cut my hair so I have decided not to go out for the swimming team."

Beaver saw the smiles of his parents disappear. They were right back where they started. The meal was eaten in a tense atmosphere with very little conversation and Wally, cheerful as ever, was the first to leave the table and Beaver suspected he was going to put some more goo on his hair before going to Mary Ellen Rogers' house.

"Ward Cleaver!" exclaimed Mrs. Cleaver as soon as Wally had gone upstairs. "I think it is high time you marched right upstairs and had this out with Wally! The idea of letting your son go around looking like that!"

"Now dear," Mr. Cleaver spoke calmly but he looked worried. "Wally is growing up. I can't just order him to change the way he wears his hair. He has good sense and he has to decide for himself."

"I can't stand it," said Mrs. Cleaver. "I simply cannot stand it."

Beaver began to wish Wally would wash the goo out of his hair so they could have a little peace around the house again. He did not want to eat any more silent meals.

"Golly," said Larry as he and Beaver went out to finish cleaning up the garage. "When my Dad comes home from a business trip there are always two or three things that he has out with my sister because she doesn't have good sense. Things like purple lipstick and gold nail polish."

The boys soon finished the job and as Larry had predicted, they found themselves with nothing to do. Somehow, having nothing to do was worse on Sunday afternoon than any other day of the week. None of their friends were home. There was nothing on television they wanted to see. Mrs. Cleaver did not want them snooping through the refrigerator eating up any of the things she planned to have for dinner. Wally had gone out so they could not tag along after him.

Finally out of boredom the boys wandered upstairs to look at Beaver's collection of old comic books.

"Hey, look at all the stuff Wally has for his hair," remarked Larry, going into the bathroom. "Enough to start a drugstore."

"This is the one that works." Beaver pointed to the

jar. "It gets hard so your hair won't bend. Like cement."

"Boy, cement hair!" Larry picked up the jar, opened it and sniffed. "It smells good, too."

"It does smell pretty good," Beaver stuck his finger in the jar and applied a dab of the stuff to his hair. Larry put a dab on his hair, too. Beaver applied a bigger dab.

"Hey, I know what!" exclaimed Larry. "Let's do our hair like Wally! It would be fun to look like a couple of creeps just for one afternoon."

"Hey, let's!" Beaver agreed except for one thing. He did not expect to look like a creep.

At last the boys had found something to do. Beaver applied a handful of the stuff to his hair and rubbed it around. Larry did the same. "Maybe we had better comb it in a hurry," suggested Beaver, picking up his comb. "I don't know how fast it hardens."

"Yeah." Larry pulled a comb out of his hip pocket and the boys went to work. They flattened their hair on top and combed it up on the sides. Rolling the ends under was difficult because they both had straight hair, but they rolled it over their fingers, patted it carefully, poked it here, prodded it there until finally they had their hair arranged in the same jellyroll fashion as Wally. They stopped to admire themselves in the mirror, and they both began to laugh.

"Boy, do we look goofy!" Larry turned his head from side to side to get the full effect.

"Yeah." Beaver studied himself and had to admit

that Larry was right. He did look goofy, but even so, he was pleased with his appearance. It was almost as if he had combed himself out of the fifth grade and into high school. He felt more grown-up, more like Wally.

"Are you sure this stuff washes out?" asked Larry. "Or do we have to chip it off?"

"Dutch Cleanser ought to take it off if soap won't." Beaver wondered if his father would wait for his own good sense to take over, too. Probably not. Fifth-graders got yelled at more than boys in high school. He knew it would be wise to keep out of his mother's sight altogether.

"Hey, I know," said Larry. "Let's go and find Wally and show him how we look."

"O.K., if we can get out of the house without Dad seeing us." Beaver was not anxious to be yelled at about his hair so soon after being yelled at about the garage.

Quietly the boys slipped down the stairs, through the dining room, into the kitchen and out the back door. Beaver found himself standing tall and walking with a swagger as they headed in the direction of Mary Ellen Rogers' house. Maybe he looked goofy to grownups and boys and girls his age, but to someone Wally's age he looked sharp and that was almost as good as being in high school. Wally was going to be pretty pleased when he saw how he was wearing his hair now.

Before the boys reached Mary Ellen Rogers' house, they saw Wally and Mary Ellen walking slowly down the street toward them. They seemed to be intensely interested in whatever they were saying to one another, and Beaver guessed that Wally had taken Mary Ellen to the drugstore for a soda. "Come on, Larry," Beaver began to run toward his brother.

"Hi, Wally," panted Beaver and put his hand to his hair. Yes, it was still in place in spite of his running. This new stuff was remarkable.

"Hi, Wally." Larry had caught up. He, too, felt his hair and found it in place.

Wally and Mary Ellen stopped and stared at the younger boys.

"How do you like it, Wally?" Beaver turned his head so Wally could see the back of his hair.

Suddenly Mary Ellen began to giggle. She looked from Beaver to Larry and back again and said, "Turn all the way around so I can see the back."

Beaver and Larry obliged, although Beaver was not sure he enjoyed being laughed at.

Larry joined Mary Ellen's laughter. "Yeah, don't we look goofy?"

Wally did not laugh. His face turned red, but he did not say anything. Beaver wondered what had gone wrong.

Then Mary Ellen turned to Wally and began to laugh even harder. "Oh, Wally . . ." She went off into a fit of giggles. "You . . . you look so funny!"

"How come?" asked Wally, bewildered. "A little while ago you thought I looked sharp."

"I know." Mary Ellen had trouble controlling her giggles. "But then Beaver and Larry came along . . ." She began to laugh again. "I'm sorry, Wally," she said when she had recovered. "It was just seeing a couple of fifth-graders . . . I guess it made me realize your hair . . . really looked funny." There she was, giggling again.

Wally managed a weak smile, but Beaver could tell he didn't really feel like smiling. Beaver was still surprised at the way things had turned out. "Come on, Larry," he said, "maybe we better go." He had a feeling Wally might have something to say to him when he returned home and he wanted to get his hair washed before Wally arrived.

Larry wanted to go home to show his hair to his sister so Beaver returned to his house alone. He opened the back door as quietly as he could and slipped inside only to find both his parents were sitting at the kitchen table drinking coffee.

"Beaver Cleaver!" His mother looked shocked when she saw his hair. "A little boy like you—"

"Beaver," said Mr. Cleaver sternly. "You march right up those stairs and wash your hair."

"Gee, Dad," protested Beaver, "aren't you going to let my own good sense take over?"

"I am not!"

"Beaver, how could you?" asked Mrs. Cleaver.

Then Wally came in through the back door. He looked just plain mad. "O.K., wise guy," he said to Beaver. "I guess you think you're pretty smart. The first time I get Mary Ellen Rogers to myself without Eddie Haskell hanging around and you have to come along and make fun of me and spoil everything."

"Gee, Wally, I wasn't trying to make fun of you,"

protested Beaver. "Honest. I thought you looked sharp and I wanted to look sharp, too."

"Ha." Wally sounded bitter.

"Well, I did." Beaver was telling the truth.

"What looks sharp on someone my age doesn't look sharp on someone your age," said Wally. "You looked just about as silly as if you went around with Dad's hat down over your ears. And you made Mary Ellen Rogers laugh. And she laughed at me, too!"

"Gee, I'm sorry, Wally." Beaver was sincere. He had not meant to make Mary Ellen laugh. "I'm going upstairs right now and wash out the goo or chip it out or whatever you have to do to get it out."

"Oh, no, you don't," said Wally. "I get the bathroom first." With one last scowl at Beaver he stomped upstairs.

"Well!" exclaimed Mrs. Cleaver with a smile as they heard the sound of water running upstairs. "I guess that takes care of Wally's hair."

"Thanks, pal!" Mr. Cleaver grinned at Beaver. "Peace around here at last!"

"You're welcome, Dad," answered Beaver and added as he listened to the water running and thought about Wally and Mary Ellen, "I guess . . ."

WALLY GOES INTO BUSINESS

The feud between Beaver and Wally began to grow worse the day Mrs. Cleaver brought home the pickles. Not that the pickles had anything to do with it. The feud had been flourishing since the day Beaver had made Mary Ellen Rogers laugh by combing his hair like Wally. First Wally would say something that would make Beaver mad and then Beaver would think up something to get back at Wally. Their parents said nothing. They hoped the boys would grow tired of their behavior and be friends again.

Mr. Cleaver came home from work carrying a large flowered china crock shaped like a barrel. "For you, dear," he said as he kissed his wife. "Pickles."

"Pickles!" exclaimed Mrs. Cleaver. "That whole big crock?"

"It is only two quarts," answered Mr. Cleaver. "We can go on lots of picnics and when the jar is empty you can use it for flowers."

"Two quarts of pickles!" Mrs. Cleaver obviously did not think the Cleaver family could eat that many pickles.

"Relax, Mom," said Wally. "I like pickles."

"So do I," said Beaver, glaring at his brother as if to say, I can eat just as many pickles as you can.

Mr. Cleaver removed the top from the crock and set it on the table. "There you are. Help yourselves."

Beaver and Wally reached toward the crock at the same time, frowned at one another and hesitated. Beaver let Wally take his pickle first because he was bigger and madder. Besides, he had felt lately that Wally would like to haul off and hit him and he wasn't taking any chances.

"Say, Dad, can I see you a minute?" asked Wally.

"What for?" asked Beaver.

"It's just something between Dad and me," answered Wally. "What do you want to know for?"

"In case it's something bad, I want to hang around and listen," answered Beaver.

"Now Beaver," said Mrs. Cleaver, "I'm sure Wally hasn't done anything bad. Have you, Wally?"

"Of course not," said Wally crossly and pulled a

slip of paper out of his pocket. "Would you sign this for me, Dad?"

"What is it?" asked Mr. Cleaver, laying his pickle on the table and reaching for the paper.

"It is just a thing so I can get a work permit," explained Wally. "Summer is going to be here before too long and I want to get out and get a job before they are all taken."

"A job!" exclaimed Mrs. Cleaver. "Oh dear—you are growing up!"

"I think that is quite a commendable project," remarked Mr. Cleaver. "Don't you, Beaver?"

"Search me, Dad—he told me to shut up and mind my own business."

Mr. Cleaver pulled out a pen and signed the slip of paper. "Good luck, Wally."

"Hey, Wally, when you go job-hunting, can I go job-hunting with you?" asked Beaver, forgetting the feud for the moment. All sorts of interesting things could happen when a boy went job-hunting. He might even find a job.

"Of course not," said Wally. "You're just a shrimp. I don't want a kid brother hanging around spoiling my chances."

"I bet you don't get a job," Beaver scowled at his brother.

Wally scowled back. "I bet I do."

"Boys!" pleaded Mrs. Cleaver.

The next afternoon Wally was late coming home from school which made Beaver suspect he was looking for a job. I'll bet he thinks he's smart, Beaver thought crossly as he watched out the window for his brother. Having to stay home while Wally looked for a job made him feel like a little brother, much littler than he really was, and he did not like the feeling. It filled him with gloom to think that no matter how old Wally was, he would always be Wally's younger brother. Just a kid brother, that was all he was and when he was eighty years old he would still be a kid brother and Wally would still think he was older and smarter and bigger and better.

A tinkling sound of bells attracted Beaver's attention. "Mom! Dad!" he shouted. "Come and look at Wally! He's coming down the street on a tricycle. And he's dressed up like a street cleaner!"

"A tricycle!" exclaimed Mrs. Cleaver. "At his age?"

Beaver and his parents rushed out to the front steps to see Wally sitting on a three-wheeled vehicle with a large box attached to the front. On the box was printed "Igloo Bars 15¢." Wally, who was wearing a white coat that was much too large for him and a coin changer on his belt, looked proud and pleased.

"Hi, Dad."

"Well, Wally, what have we here?" asked Mr. Cleaver.

"It's my new job. I'm selling Igloo Bars after school and all summer," he answered.

"Riding a tricycle at your age," scoffed envious Beaver.

"Bicycle," corrected Wally.

"It has three wheels so it is a tricycle." Beaver knew he was right.

"Bicycle!" Wally hoped to end the argument by raising his voice.

"Wally, you ought to make them give you a jacket that fits," said Mrs. Cleaver to change the subject. "You look lost in that one."

"Most of the fellows are bigger," explained Wally. "This was the closest they had to my size."

Beaver walked over to the cart and examined it more closely. Wally was lucky to be old enough to ride around ringing bells and selling ice cream and making change. Beaver lifted the lid of the ice box to look in. Vapor from the dry ice rose in a cloud.

"Hey, get your nose out of my ice box," ordered Wally. "Dad, I sold three of them on the way home."

"Oh, you're working already?" Mr. Cleaver seemed pleased that Wally had wasted no time.

"Uh . . . Dad?" Wally was embarrassed about something.

"Yes, Wally?"

"Well, there are a . . . couple of things." Wally hesitated. "I have to give the man a twenty-five dollar deposit on the bike in case something happens to it and I need two dollars for dry ice."

"That's fine, Wally. I'll lend it to you," agreed Mr. Cleaver, "but remember, I'll expect to be paid back."

"Sure, Dad. I'll pay you back out of my profits," said Wally. "The man said some fellows make as much as thirty-five dollars a week."

"Hey, Wally," said Beaver as his parents went into the house. "That's pretty good. You've only been working an hour and already you've got twenty-seven dollars."

"Yes, but I've got to pay it back," Wally pointed out.

Beaver lifted the lid of the ice box and peered in. "Where are the vanilla ones?" he asked.

"You cut that out," said Wally. "I'm the only one allowed to stick my hand in there. It's a Board of Health law."

"Well then stick your hand in there and give me a vanilla one."

"Yeah?" Wally shut the lid of the ice box. "You stick your hand in your pocket and give me fifteen cents."

"Aw, Wally," protested Beaver. "You know me. I'm your brother."

"I don't care," answered Wally. "I have to pay for these at the end of the week. Anyway you've got a drawer full of money upstairs."

Beaver was annoyed. "O.K., be that way. I wouldn't buy any Igloo Bar from someone who wouldn't give his own brother a free one." With that he turned and went into the house.

The next afternoon after school Beaver did not have any trouble finding Wally. He heard the bell of the Igloo Bar cart and followed its sound until he saw Wally pedalling slowly down the street. Beaver caught up with him and began to jog along behind.

Wally stopped and turned around. "Look, Beaver —do you have to follow me every place I go?"

"This is a public sidewalk," Beaver informed his brother. "I've got just as much right on it as you have." He did not intend to admit to Wally that he hoped someone from his class would see them together and learn that his brother was an Igloo man. No, he wouldn't give Wally the satisfaction of knowing he was secretly proud of him.

"Well, just keep out of my way when I'm selling stuff," said Wally. "It gives me the creeps to have you tagging along."

Beaver dropped two paces behind and continued to jog along after Wally who soon stopped when two girls about Beaver's age approached him. They bought a chocolate and a vanilla Igloo Bar.

"Hi, Peggy," said Beaver to one of the girls. "That's my brother selling ice cream bars."

For some reason this sent the girls into a gale of giggles.

Wally turned red. "What did you go and say that for?" he demanded when the girls had left. "How would you like to have a kid brother following you around."

"That would be neat," said Beaver, hoping to annoy Wally. "If I had a kid brother I would like him to like me. I would be real nice to him and give him a free Igloo Bar every time he wanted one. You wouldn't catch me acting like I thought I was a big shot just because I was riding around on a tricycle."

"Look, will you beat it and stop being a wise guy?" Wally made a fist as if he were about to get off and punch Beaver. Instead he started ringing the bell and pedalling down the street. Beaver jogged along behind him.

Then the boys met Wally's friends Eddie, Tooey and Chester.

"Hey, look who's here in full dress uniform—Captain Igloo in person!" Eddie clicked his heels and saluted.

"Hi, Wally," said Chester. "I didn't know there was an Eskimo navy."

"Don't just stand there," said Eddie. "Salute him."

Chester and Tooey clicked their heels and saluted. "Aye, aye, sir," said Tooey.

Wally was embarrassed. "Aw, cut it out, will you, Eddie?"

Beaver began to feel a little sorry for Wally—but not sorry enough to stop jogging along after him.

"Come on, fellows, what will you have?" asked Eddie. "This is my treat."

When the boys gave their order Wally reached in the ice box, pulled out three Igloo Bars and handed them around. The boys all peeled back the wrappers and took a bite.

"Hey, Eddie," said Wally. "That will be forty-five cents."

"Gee, I didn't bring my money with me today. How about trusting me until tomorrow?" said Eddie.

"Gee, I don't know, Eddie." Wally was doubtful. "I'm not allowed to do that."

"O.K., fellows," said Eddie to Tooey and Chester. "Put them back."

Wally looked miserably at the three Igloo Bars, each with one bite missing. "Well . . . just make sure you pay me tomorrow."

"Carry on, Admiral!" said Tooey. The three boys saluted and went on down the street, eating their unpaid-for Igloo Bars.

Now Beaver really did feel sorry for Wally. "Gee,

Wally, that was sure tough. You shouldn't have let that creep Eddie Haskell get away with that."

Wally turned on the seat of the bicycle. "Why don't you mind your own business?" he said angrily. "I can take care of my business without any help from you." Then he continued pedalling along, ringing his bell and looking for business.

Larry Mondello was the next customer. "Hi, Wally," he said. "Hi, Beaver. You're sure lucky to have a brother in the Igloo Bar business. I bet you get all you want free."

"He does not," corrected Wally. "He has to pay for them just like anyone else." Wally had felt even less enthusiasm than usual for Larry since the day Mary Ellen Rogers laughed at his haircomb.

"Sure," said Beaver. "I haven't had a single Igloo Bar all afternoon. I could starve to death before my own brother would give me one little old Igloo Bar."

Larry thought this was too bad. "Have one on me," he said. "And I'm pretty hungry. I can eat two. A chocolate and a pistachio."

"Do you have any money?" Wally asked suspiciously.

Larry sounded hurt. "Sure I have money. I'm on my way to the store for my mother."

Wally handed over the Igloo Bars, two for Larry and one for Beaver, and the boys began to eat.

"The money, Larry," reminded Wally. "Remember?"

"Oh, sure." Cheerfully Larry reached in his pocket and pulled out a ten dollar bill.

Wally's face fell. "Gee, I don't have change for a ten," he admitted.

"I'll give you the money the first thing tomorrow," promised Larry.

This information did not seem to cheer Wally. "O.K., just be sure that you do," he said and started pedalling down the street.

"I'll remind Larry if he forgets," promised Beaver as he followed Wally. Poor old Wally, he was having his troubles this afternoon and Beaver felt responsible for Larry's behavior. After all, Larry was his friend and he did not want him to get Wally in trouble because then Wally really would be mad. Look at the way he acted when Larry combed his hair up instead of down for a change.

"For the last time, get lost, will you?" Wally was really angry. "You see the kind of luck you bring me. Now beat it!"

"O.K., O.K." Now Beaver was getting angry himself, because Wally was angry and the funny part of it was, he knew the real reason Wally acted the way he did was that he was embarrassed because he wasn't a better businessman and did not want Beaver to know it. Feeling angry and sorry at the same time, Beaver turned and left Wally to pedal down the street alone.

That evening the brothers ignored one another as much as possible. Beaver read a book but as he looked up from time to time, he noticed that Wally, who was supposed to be studying history, spent a lot of time figuring on a piece of paper. He looked worried. Good, thought Beaver crossly. I'm glad he's worried—then he won't think he's so good just because he's old enough to be in business.

Then Beaver thought of the money Larry owed Wally and he did not feel so pleased with Wally's problems. Wally did not look proud any more. He looked worried and unhappy and Beaver felt sorry for him—even if he was mad at him.

The next day after school Beaver went home and found his mother trying to make room for a large carton of Igloo Bars in the freezer.

"Oh, hello, Beaver," she said. "I thought you were going with Wally this afternoon."

"He told me he would clop me one if I followed him," said Beaver. "I saw him, though. A bunch of high school girls were hanging around him giggling." Beaver had seen enough to know that Wally was pretty uncomfortable. He had looked red and embarrassed. The girls had been squealing about how cute Wally looked in his white coat and a couple of them were reaching into the ice box and Wally was too bashful to tell them about the Health Department rule. There was one girl who was not giggling and that was Mary Ellen Rogers. This made it harder for Wally to sit on his tricycle and be giggled at.

"Would you like an Igloo Bar?" Mrs. Cleaver asked Beaver. "I'll pay for it."

"Uh uh," said Beaver. "I wouldn't eat one of those crummy old bars of Wally's even if I was starving out on the desert with my tongue hanging out."

"How about a pickle instead?" suggested Mrs. Cleaver.

"I think I'd rather have a salami sandwich."

Beaver opened the breadbox. "And you know what? I bet old Wally can't even collect from those girls."

"Now see here, Beaver," said Mrs. Cleaver as she shoved the last of the Igloo Bars into the freezer. "You boys have been wrangling for the last two days. I think it's time you made up. You should remember all the nice things Wally has done for you. He helped you learn to bat and he lets you sleep in his sleeping bag sometimes and when you have a bad dream he lets you climb into his bed."

"I'll make up if he makes up first," Beaver told his mother.

At dinner Beaver and Wally ignored one another. Both Mr. and Mrs. Cleaver tried to make conversation with their sons who answered in monosyllables.

Finally Mrs. Cleaver said brightly, "Well, Wally, were you able to collect from the girls this afternoon or did you treat them to Igloo Bars?"

Wally threw down his napkin, glared at Beaver and said, "You little sneak!" Then he left the table, stomped upstairs and slammed the bedroom door leaving his family to look after him in astonished silence.

Mr. Cleaver cleared his throat. "Well, it appears that Wally didn't collect from the girls."

"I think I'll do my homework downstairs tonight," remarked Beaver. "Wally's been acting like such a big shot ever since he got the job and he's been so mean to me I'm being mean right back to him."

"I don't think you should go out of your way to be mean to him, but you certainly have as much right to be in that room as he does," said Mr.

Cleaver. "And you can march right up and tell him so."

"Yes, sir," answered Beaver.

"But don't annoy Wally while he's figuring his accounts," cautioned Mrs. Cleaver. "Mr. Nibling is coming to collect tomorrow."

When Beaver entered the room he shared with his brother, Wally turned from his desk. "I thought I told you to leave me alone."

"Dad said this room is as much my room as yours," answered Beaver. "And if you don't let me stay here he's going to come up and hit you."

"Aw, he didn't say that," muttered Wally, turning back to his accounts.

"What are you doing, calling Dad a liar?" Beaver knew when he spoke that he was exaggerating, but the way Wally had been acting lately, he had to say something.

"Will you keep quiet? I'm having trouble," said Wally. "Mr. Nibling is coming to collect tomorrow and I'm three dollars and seventy-five cents short."

"Tough," said Beaver.

"And not only that, I'm not going to have the five dollars to pay back Dad for the bicycle," said Wally.

"Tougher," said Beaver. "And it's a tricycle."

Wally ignored the remark about the tricycle. "Beaver, you got nine dollars saved up. How about lending me some money?" he asked.

"Why should I?" asked Beaver.

"Because I'm short," answered Wally.

"Then why don't you collect from all the people who owe you money?" asked Beaver.

"Boy, you're a rat," remarked Wally.

"Yeah," agreed Beaver cheerfully. "But I'm a rat with nine dollars."

On Saturday morning Wally left immediately after breakfast to start his Igloo Bar route. He did not say so, but Beaver knew he hoped to take in enough money before Mr. Nibling came to collect to pay off his debts. Why else would Wally leave without eating a second helping of hotcakes? Beaver mopped up a pool of syrup with a piece of hotcake and looked outside at the weather. The day was cloudy and from the movement of the trees he could tell there was a stiff breeze blowing. It was not a good day for selling ice cream bars which served old Wally right. Beaver, sitting in the warm kitchen, chewed the syrupy bite of hotcake and pictured Wally, shivering in the white jacket that was too big for him, as he pedalled through the streets of Mayfield ringing his bell to advertise the Igloo Bars that no one wanted to buy right after breakfast on such a cold morning. He would pedal and pedal and ring and ring, but no one would come near him. Beaver guessed old Wally wouldn't look so smart *this* morning, but somehow, the picture did not give him the satisfaction he had hoped.

Beaver was still sitting at the breakfast table when Larry Mondello arrived. "Boy, do those hotcakes smell good!" remarked Larry hopefully.

"Sorry, Larry," said Mrs. Cleaver. "Beaver is eating the last hotcake. How would you like a nice pickle?"

"No, thank you, Mrs. Cleaver. I'm not supposed to

eat between meals." Larry sat down at the table across from Beaver anyway. "Say, Beaver," he said, "how about lending me forty-five cents?"

"What for?" asked Beaver.

"To pay Wally for those Igloo Bars we ate. Two for me and one for you," answered Larry. "He just came to our house and asked me for the money."

Beaver began to feel just a little bit sorry for Wally, riding around on his tricycle, shivering in the white jacket, while he tried to collect from Larry for three Igloo Bars. Sorry and ashamed that an Igloo Bar he had eaten was still not paid for. "How come you haven't paid him before this?" he asked.

Larry looked embarrassed. "Well . . . my mother won't give me the money. On account I'm sort of overweight I'm not supposed to eat stuff like that between meals and she won't give me the money because she says I have to learn a lesson. Come on, Beaver, lend me the money. Wally says he's got to have it this morning before Mr. Nibling comes to collect."

Poor Wally, thought Beaver. Probably he was pedalling around on his tricycle as fast as he could trying to collect from a lot of people like Eddie Haskell and all those giggling girls who wouldn't pay. Well it just served him right for thinking he was so smart because he had a job . . . but it also showed how good-natured he was, letting people have Igloo Bars without paying. Beaver himself had eaten one of the ice cream bars. "Sure, Larry," he finally agreed. "I'll lend you the money."

"Gee, thanks," said Larry. "I guess Wally is having

a bad time. He must not be a very good businessman."

"My brother is a good businessman," contradicted
Beaver, getting up from the table. "It is people who
say they will pay and don't that cause the trouble."
It was all right for Beaver to criticize Wally because
he was related to him, but he did not want Larry
doing it, too. Who was Larry to criticize Wally,
anyway? Larry owed him forty-five cents.

"Beaver, do you think Wally is really in trouble
with his route?" Mrs. Cleaver sounded concerned.
"He did seem angry when I asked him if he treated
the girls and I was only joking."

Beaver glanced at Larry. "Who, Wally?" he asked.
"Why should he be in trouble?"

Beaver was halfway up the stairs when the doorbell rang. When Mrs. Cleaver opened it, he saw a
man whom he guessed at once to be Mr. Nibling.

"Is Wally Cleaver in? I have come to collect,"
said the man, confirming Beaver's guess. He was
impatient-looking and Beaver was glad he did not
have to sell Igloo Bars for Mr. Nibling.

"Why . . . he's out on his route right now," answered Mrs. Cleaver. "I don't think he expected you
quite this early."

"I told that boy I would be here at nine o'clock
on the dot." Mr. Nibling glanced at his watch. "And
it is now six minutes after nine."

There was something about the way Mr. Nibling
called Wally "that boy" that Beaver did not like.
"It's O.K., Mom," answered Beaver. "The money
is in his top drawer. I'll get it." He ran upstairs to

the bedroom where he yanked open his own drawer and took out seven dollars. Then he opened Wally's drawer and took out the money Wally had spent so much time counting the night before. Then he ran downstairs and handed Mr. Nibling the money. "Here you are, Mr. Nibling," he said.

"You mean Wally really had the money?" whispered Larry.

Beaver frowned at Larry instead of answering.

Mr. Nibling counted the money and looked as if he were surprised to find it all there. He counted it a second time to make sure.

"May I please have a receipt?" asked Beaver, feeling that someone in the family should be a good businessman. He pocketed the receipt, thanked Mr. Nibling who said he would talk to Wally later, and when the man had gone, Beaver and Larry went upstairs and played checkers until Larry had to go home. Then Beaver sat on his bed thinking up ways to put off cleaning his half of the room until he heard the back door open.

"Hey, Mom," Wally called. "Was Mr. Nibling here yet?"

"Oh yes, a long time ago," Beaver heard his mother answer. "He picked up the money and said he would talk to you later."

"Gee whiz, where'd he get my money from?" Beaver heard Wally ask his mother.

"Beaver got it for him," answered Mrs. Cleaver. "He said he knew it was in your top drawer."

"Boy, what a dirty trick!" Wally said and Beaver heard him coming up the stairs two at a time. He burst into the room and glared at Beaver. "Hey, you little wise guy!"

"Hi, Wally," answered Beaver calmly.

"Don't 'hi' me." Wally was really angry. "How come you went and gave Mr. Nibling my ice cream money?"

"Because he came and asked for it." Beaver got up from the bed and began to straighten his half of the top of the dresser. He moved the miniature totem pole to the exact center. That was the dividing line.

"You knew I was seven dollars short and if I'd have been here, I could have explained it to him. Now he's going to call me back and fire me and everything." Wally sat wearily down on his bed. "I sure hope it makes you happy," he said bitterly.

Silently Beaver handed his brother a slip of paper.

Wally looked at it and read, " 'Paid in full' . . . But I was a whole seven dollars short and . . . Hey, Beaver, you didn't make up the difference, did you?"

"Well, I did kind of put some of my money in there," admitted Beaver. "But you can pay me back sometime when you get around to it. No hurry."

"Gee, how come?" asked Wally. "I thought you were sore at me and thought I was a rat."

Beaver thought it over. Why had he helped Wally out? He had been mad at him—or had he?

"Well, I did think you were a rat, sort of," said Beaver at last, "but I knew the man would be mad at you because you didn't have all his money. I

don't mind you looking like a rat to me, but I don't
want you looking like a rat to other people."

"Boy, this is the neatest thing you ever did, especially when you were sore at me for telling you to
get lost." Wally, it seemed to Beaver, was smiling
for the first time since he had taken the Igloo Bar
route.

"I guess I wasn't really sore at you," confessed
Beaver. "I guess I was just feeling bad because you
didn't want me around."

"I'm sorry, Beaver," said Wally, "but figure it out.
You can't always be hanging around me when I
grow up and go to college and get married."

"I know," agreed Beaver, "but I don't want to
hang around you when you go to college and get
married. I just want to hang around you when you
sell Igloo Bars."

Wally gave Beaver a playful shove. "O.K., you
can hang around me all you want while I'm selling
Igloo Bars but not when I go to college and get
married. And if you ever get in a jam and I can
help you out, let me know." He started out the
door. "Aren't you coming with me?" he asked.

Beaver pulled his jacket out of the closet and
started to follow Wally who was singing, " 'If you're
ever up a tree, call on me,' " as he ran down the
stairs.

At the top of the stairs Beaver stopped, leaned
over the bannister railing and called out to Wally.
"Thanks anyway Wally. I don't think I'll come
today." Tagging after Wally wasn't going to be half
as much fun now that Wally said he could.

BEAVER MAKES A LOAN

The Mayfield School P.T.A. was planning a carnival to raise money to buy a record player and some new records for the teachers to use in the classrooms. Beaver had been trying to save his money so he would have some to spend at the different booths, but somehow, something always seemed to happen that required money—he was extra-hungry on a Saturday afternoon and really needed an ice cream soda or there was an extra-good movie about a mechanical monster or a mad scientist playing and all the other fellows were going. There was always something and now it was nearly time for the carnival and Beaver had almost no money left and certainly not enough to buy the twenty-five cent notebook he needed for school.

"Hey, Mom, can I have a quarter for a new notebook for school?" Beaver asked one morning at breakfast.

"I don't have a quarter, Beaver," answered Mrs. Cleaver. "Maybe you can catch your father. He's just backing the car out now."

"Dad! Hey, Dad!" Beaver yelled out the back door.

Mr. Cleaver stopped the car by the back steps. "Yes, Beaver?"

"I need a quarter for a notebook," explained Beaver.

His father reached into his pocket and pulled out a handful of small change and a couple of crumpled bills. "I don't have a quarter, but here—take this dollar and bring back seventy-five cents."

Beaver accepted the money. "Thanks, Dad. I'll bring back the change."

"Be sure you do," said Mr. Cleaver as he continued backing down the driveway.

When Beaver got on the school bus that morning he sat down beside Larry. "Did you remember to bring your notebook?" he asked.

Larry groaned. "I forgot and I bet Miss Landers will just about kill me. Did you bring yours?"

"No, but as soon as I get to school I'm going to run across the street to the store and buy one. I guess it is better to risk being late to school than to go without the notebook. Miss Landers has reminded us enough." Beaver pulled the dollar bill out of his pocket.

"Gee, a whole dollar," Larry looked envious. "How about lending me some of it so I can get a notebook, too?"

"It's not my dollar," said Beaver. "I promised to bring home the change."

"But Beaver, I get my allowance tomorrow and I'll pay you right back," coaxed Larry. "You don't want to be a mean guy and get me in trouble, do you?"

"Well—" Naturally Beaver did not want to get a friend in trouble.

"I tell you what," said Larry as the bus pulled into the school grounds. "Let me take the dollar and I'll whiz over to the school store and get both notebooks. That way you won't have to take a chance on being late. And I'll slip your notebook and fifty cents to you as soon as I get back. Miss Landers won't ask for them until after the pledge allegiance."

"O.K., Larry," agreed Beaver, glad that he would not have to risk being late. Miss Landers had spoken to him about this twice last week.

So Larry took the dollar bill and ran across the street as soon as the bus stopped, while Beaver, glad that he was going to be on time and have his notebook, too, went on into the classroom. In the midst of the flag salute Larry, red and panting, ar-

rived and dropped a notebook on Beaver's desk on
his way to his own seat. Miss Landers frowned.

Beaver wondered about his change but decided
that Larry would give it to him later. Probably he
had not wanted to risk having it roll off Beaver's
desk and down the aisle during the flag salute. When
everyone was seated, Miss Landers suggested that
the class be thinking of ideas for their booth at the
P.T.A. carnival. The sixth-grade was going to have
a fortune-telling booth, the fourth grade was going
to sell taffy apples. It was up to the fifth grade to
think of a better idea. Beaver forgot about his change
until recess when he noticed that Larry was not
around. Beaver began to look for him and finally
found Larry down in the basement by the door to
the cafeteria.

"What are you doing down here?" demanded
Beaver.

"Oh, just thinking," answered Larry.

"You forgot to give me my change," said Beaver.

"Change?" said Larry. "Oh, yeah. Change. Well,
I . . . uh . . . don't have it."

"How come?" demanded Beaver as the bell rang
for the boys and girls to return to their classrooms.

"Well—Mr. Prouty over at the store told me I
owed him fifty cents from before and he wouldn't
let me buy anything till I paid it. So I had to give
him the whole dollar," confessed Larry.

"But that was my father's dollar," said Beaver.
"I've got to have the change."

"But golly, Beaver, I did it for you," protested
Larry. "If you didn't have a notebook, you'd be in

trouble, and if you were late to class, you'd be in trouble, and I didn't want to see you get in trouble because you're my pal. Come on, Beaver, we better get to class."

"What do you mean, you didn't want to get me in trouble?" demanded Beaver. "Now you've really got me in trouble because my dad is lots fiercer than Miss Landers. What am I going to tell him?"

Larry looked hurt. "Gee, Beaver, I was just trying to help you," he said.

"Some help you turned out to be," said Beaver crossly.

"I get my allowance tomorrow," said Larry. "I'll bring you the money then. Honest. Cross my heart and hope to die."

"You better," muttered Beaver and wondered what he would tell his father in the meantime. Mr. Cleaver was not the kind of father who would forget seventy-five cents.

He did not have to wait long to find out. When Mr. Cleaver came home from work that day he kissed Mrs. Cleaver and held out his hand to Beaver.

"You want something, Dad?" Beaver tried to look innocent.

"My change, Beaver," answered his father.

There was nothing for Beaver to do but explain and as he expected, his father looked displeased.

"Well, Beaver," said Mr. Cleaver. "All I know is that you owe me seventy-five cents. You're supposed to get your movie money tomorrow, but now you just won't get it."

"But gee, Dad, it's a real neat picture and all

the fellows are going," said Beaver, "and the money
I had left I was going to spend at the school carnival
next week because it is to raise money for a new
phonograph and records for the school. Miss Landers
says it is a worthy cause."

Mr. Cleaver remained unmoved. "If as you say
Larry owes you seventy-five cents, you just get it
from him if you want to go to the movies. And
anything left over you can use toward the worthy
cause."

"He promised it to me tomorrow," said Beaver.

"Huh!" exclaimed Wally who had come into the
kitchen and was listening to the conversation. "Did
he ever give you back that Scout knife he borrowed?"

"Well, no," admitted Beaver, "but he had a good
excuse."

"How about your baseball cap?" asked Wally.

"He had a good excuse for that, too," said Beaver.

"Sure," said Wally. "And you know what I'll bet
Larry's doing right now? I'll bet he's sitting over at
his house right now thinking up a good excuse for
not paying you back the seventy-five cents."

"You just wait until tomorrow," said Beaver, but
he was beginning to have misgivings. Wally might
be right. Larry was the kind of boy who spent more
time thinking up reasons for not doing things than
he would spend actually doing them.

But the next morning Larry telephoned. "Hello,
Beaver—I got your seventy-five cents and I'm coming
right over to pay you back so if you're going to go
anywhere, stay there."

"Sure, Larry," agreed Beaver cheerfully and when he had hung up he turned to Wally and his father and said with an I-told-you-so note in his voice, "Larry's coming over to pay me back the money so I can go to the movies." Tactfully he refrained from adding, "So there!"

"I'll believe it when I see it," said Wally.

Beaver ignored his brother. "It's a neat movie about a mad scientist who makes a mechanical man that will do anything he wants it to." Then he went out to sit on the front steps to wait for Larry, and while he waited, he planned to go to the movie early, buy a bag of popcorn and get a seat in the front row. He waited and waited.

Wally came out in his white uniform on his way to start his Igloo Bar route. "If Larry double-crossed you, I'll lend you the money to go to the movies."

"He didn't double-cross me," said Beaver. "He's on his way over to pay me the money now."

"He was on his way over an hour ago," Wally pointed out and went on down the street.

Beaver began to be uneasy so he decided the thing to do was telephone Larry and find out what was delaying him. Perhaps his mother had made him clean up his room before he left. Or more likely she was making him stay in his room for pestering his sister. It was Mrs. Mondello who answered the telephone. She said that Larry had left two hours ago for Beaver's house.

"I wonder what could have happened to him," remarked Mrs. Cleaver who guessed from Beaver's

side of the conversation that Larry had started even
if he had not arrived.

"Maybe a lion got loose from the circus and ate
him up," said Beaver gloomily.

Mrs. Cleaver merely laughed at this ridiculous
suggestion.

"Maybe he got amnesia in his head and he's
walking around and doesn't even know he's Larry,"
suggested Beaver, not believing it himself.

Beaver spent a long, lonely afternoon. He still
wanted to believe in Larry, but his faith was shaken.
No real disaster could befall Larry on the streets of
Mayfield and the only reason he did not come was
that he had lost the money or had forgotten. He
thought about Larry and he thought about the
movie he was missing, a movie with a mad scientist
and a mechanical monster in the same picture. The
poster outside the theater showed the monster step-
ping on the United Nations building. There were
three Popeye cartoons, too . . .

The worst of it was Beaver's mother and father
began to look sympathetic as the afternoon wore
on. They kept exchanging looks that said quite
plainly, Poor Beaver. He trusted his friend and look
what happened. Finally Mr. Cleaver said, "Beav,
I'm sorry about the way Larry let you down."

Beaver made an effort to defend his friend. "Oh,
he didn't let me down. He started with the money
but something must have happened to him." He
knew he was not convincing his father—how could
he? He could not make himself believe what he was
saying.

"Well, I'm sure it will work out," said Mr. Cleaver. "And in the meantime, I wonder if you could do me a big favor. How about running down to the drugstore and getting me a paper? And while you are there you can get yourself a soda."

Beaver knew his father was trying to do something that would cheer him up. "Sure, Dad," he said with what he hoped was enthusiasm. At the door he turned and said to his father, "Say, Dad—when Larry gets here, tell him I'll be right back."

"Sure, Beav." Mr. Cleaver spoke much too heartily.

Beaver felt better just getting out of the house. The afternoon was warm and sunny and he ran down the street pretending he was running ninety yards for a touchdown while a stadium full of people cheered. By the time Beaver reached the drugstore he felt light-hearted once more and Larry and the seventy-five cents no longer seemed so important. Sure, Larry would return it sometime so why worry about it. In the meantime he would enjoy a soda.

He pushed open the door of the drugstore and headed for the soda fountain when he heard a familiar voice—Larry's voice. He stopped behind a rack of comic books to listen.

Larry, seated at the counter with an ice cream soda in front of him, was saying, "How do you suppose they work it when the mechanical monster steps on a man and squashes him?"

"Aw, they don't squash a real man," answered Whitey. "They use a dummy."

Gilbert had a different theory. "They do it with trick photography."

Then Whitey asked, "Are you going to have another soda, Larry?"

With his own ears Beaver heard Larry say, "No, I can't. I already spent the whole seventy-five cents."

The whole seventy-five cents! Beaver's seventy-five cents. The long lonely, miserable day came back to Beaver . . . the hours he had sat on the front steps . . . the way Wally scoffed and then offered to lend him money . . . the unwanted sympathy of his mother and father . . . That Larry. That no-good double-crossing Larry! And all the time he was enjoying a good movie and lapping up a soda on Beaver's money. Beaver was mad, just plain mad. He was so mad he wished . . . he wished a mechanical monster would come along and squash Larry, that's what he wished. Squash him flat like a bug.

But since there was no mechanical monster around to handle the situation, it was up to Beaver to take care of it himself.

Beaver stalked out from behind the comic book rack and advanced toward the three boys seated at the counter as Larry was saying, "Boy, that was the neatest movie I ever saw. When the monster reached up and grabbed the rockets . . ." Larry, looking in the mirror, saw Beaver standing behind him. ". . . right out of the air." He turned around on his stool and said weakly, "Hi, Beaver."

"Hi, Larry," said Beaver with a scowl. He wished he was wearing a couple of six-shooters like someone in a Western. Then old Larry would be scared.

"Uh . . . where've you been all day?" asked Larry.

"Waiting at my house for you to show up," answered Beaver. "Just like you told me to."

"Gee, Beaver," said Larry, trying to explain. "I was on my way over and then I met Gilbert and Whitey and then I had to go to the movies with them."

Had to go to the movies with them. Boy, that was a good one. "Larry Mondello," said Beaver. "You come outside with me."

"Gee, Beaver, you wouldn't sock a fellow with a stomach full of soda, would you?" pleaded Larry.

"I sure would," answered Beaver with relish. "I would sock him hard."

Larry managed to grin. "But don't forget, Beaver —there's three of us."

"I'm not fighting anybody," said Gilbert.

"Me neither," said Whitey. "I'm not mad at anybody."

"I'm not mad, either." Larry looked hopefully at Beaver. "Me and Beaver are practically best friends."

Beaver was unmoved by this display of friendship. "Come on, Larry."

"I don't have to leave here if I don't want to," Larry told Beaver. "And if you start something in here, you'll get in big trouble with Mr. Peabody."

"O.K., Larry." Beaver looked as menacing as he knew how. "But now I know what you are. You are a rat, that's what you are, and I'm not going to speak to you again as long as I live because you're such a big rat." And with that Beaver turned and walked out of the drugstore without stopping for a soda. He was halfway home before he remembered that he had not bought a paper for his father either, but he knew it did not matter. His father had not really wanted the paper. He had only wanted to do something to cheer up Beaver.

With considerable relish Beaver thought of a lot of other things Larry had done, too. The time he had bought the Igloo Bars from Wally and didn't have the change and how he hadn't believed Wally had a letterman's sweater and how he had not been anxious to help clean up the garage when they built the chinchilla cages.

Well, he would fix Larry, Beaver decided on the way home. He would start a club. That's what he would do. He would go get a bunch of the fellows, Whitey and Gilbert and Harold and somebody else, together and they would form a club. There was an old abandoned car in a vacant lot that they could use for a clubhouse . . . for regular meetings . . . for initiations they would use somebody's basement because they would need a place that was real dark and secret. They would think up a real good initiation with solemn oaths to swear and maybe they could even write their names in blood. They would call their club the Bloody five . . . except maybe they would have more than five members. Maybe The Fiends would be a better name. The Bloody Fiends! That was it. That was a keen name for a club. And the purpose of the Bloody Fiends would be just one thing. To keep Larry out!

Beaver knew that if the club was to keep Larry out, they would have to do something to make him want to get in. They would all wear some kind of armband, he decided, and they would have a special mysterious handshake they would use whenever they met which would be pretty often because they were all in the same room at school. Larry would see the armbands and see them all shaking hands all the time and he would begin to wonder what was going on and when he asked around, all the kids at school would say "Did you know? They are members of the Bloody Fiends. It is a very exclusive club."

And then Larry would say, "Hey, fellows, how about letting me be a Bloody Fiend?" And they would all say, "Nope. To be a Bloody Fiend you have to be a good guy. And you, Larry Mondello, are not a good guy. You are a bad guy." And Larry would slink away and hang his head. But he wouldn't give up, because it wouldn't be any fun for Beaver if he gave up. No sir, Larry would still want to be a member of the Bloody Fiends. He would want to be a member more than he had ever wanted anything in his whole life.

Beaver tried to think what Larry would do next. Maybe he would get his mother to ask Beaver if he could join the club. Mrs. Mondello would come to Beaver and beg him with tears in her eyes to let Larry join the club and Beaver would just smile mysteriously and say he was sorry but Larry was not good enough to be a Bloody Fiend. And then Mrs. Mondello would go to his mother and ask her to make Beaver let Larry into the club and his mother would say that she was sorry, too, but Larry was not qualified to be a member of the club. Then Larry would *really* feel terrible. He would slink around, hanging his head in shame because he wasn't good enough to be a Bloody Fiend.

And for the first time that day Beaver felt really cheerful.

Beaver had not been home long when the doorbell rang.

"Hey, Beav!" Wally yelled up the stairs. "Larry wants to see you."

"Tell him to go away," Beaver yelled back.

"He says he wants to see you," Wally shouted up the stairs.

"Ask him if he wants a punch in the nose," Beaver shouted back.

"No, he doesn't want a punch in the nose," called Wally. "He wants to give you the seventy-five cents and tell you he is sorry."

Then Beaver heard his mother say, "For goodness sake, boys, stop all this shouting. Larry, you just go right on upstairs and talk to Beaver yourself."

While Larry and Wally were climbing the stairs Beaver had time to look in the mirror and rehearse a really threatening expression. Jaw set . . . eyes half-closed . . . fists clenched.

"Uh . . . hi, Beaver." Larry looked thoroughly apologetic. "Gee, I'm sorry. I know I am a big rat and I shouldn't have done what I did, but I just sort of . . . got carried away when I was talking to the fellows. You . . . you know how it is."

"I know how *you* are."

"Gee, Beaver, I felt so awful I told my Dad about it. He gave me the money to give to you and he told me I couldn't go to the movies for a whole month." Larry looked hopefully at Beaver.

"You can leave the money on the dresser on your way out," said Beaver.

Larry laid a fifty-cent piece and a quarter on the dresser. Then he laid a sack of marbles beside the money. "I . . . I brought you my best marbles, too."

"No, thank you," said Beaver. "I've got my own marbles."

Larry appeared not to know what to say next. "Well . . . uh . . . goodby . . . I guess." He turned and started down the stairs leaving the money and his best marbles behind.

"Golly, Beaver," said Wally when Larry had gone. "What did you act that way for? He said he was sorry."

"Because he's a rat," said Beaver.

"O.K., O.K.," said Wally. "So Larry is a rat. Why don't you forget it? You got your seventy-five cents back, didn't you?"

"Aw, that Larry . . ." was all Beaver would say. And the truth of the matter was that he had begun to enjoy being mad at Larry.

BEAVER'S BABY PICTURE

Beaver soon discovered that not speaking to Larry was hard work. Larry was everyplace—on the school bus, in the classroom, on the playground. Beaver also discovered that no one was interested in forming a secret club to keep Larry out. They thought it would be a good idea to have a club sometime, and the Bloody Fiends was a good name for the club, but why keep Larry out? There was nothing wrong with Larry. He was fat and a little slow, but everybody liked him because he was always good-natured. He was funny, too. Anyway, all the boys were too

125

busy thinking about the school carnival to plan about
a club right now. There was plenty of time during
summer vacation.

The worst of it was that the whole class, although
they felt Larry should not have gone to the movies
and drunk a soda on Beaver's money, thought
Beaver should forget the whole thing now that the
money had been returned, and after a few days of
not speaking to Larry, Beaver soon discovered the
whole thing was a bore. He wanted to forget it, too,
but after behaving the way he had, he did not
know how to start speaking to Larry.

Not speaking was particularly difficult when the
class was trying to plan its booth for the carnival.
Larry would say something and Beaver would start
to agree until he remembered he was not speaking.
The class discussed a popcorn booth, a balloon-
popping booth and a booth for dousing candle
flames with water pistols. This last was a good idea,
they all agreed, until they learned the other fifth-
grade class had had the same idea first. They finally
settled on an idea that pleased almost everyone—a
baby-picture guessing booth. Each member of the
class was to bring to school a baby picture with his
name on the back. The pictures would be tacked
up in the booth and everyone who paid ten cents
and could guess correctly who ten of the babies
were would win a yo-yo.

Everyone had something to say. One boy said it
might not work because all babies looked alike.
Most of the girls scoffed at this idea. Judy Haskell
raised her hand and said, "I have a baby picture that

was taken in color. My mother was going to send it to Hollywood so I would get to be a movie star but she loved me too much to let me go."

The entire class laughed at this and Beaver reminded himself to be sure and ask his mother to find a baby picture to contribute to the booth. She had a whole album full of his baby pictures—Beaver in his playpen. Beaver pulling a cat's tail. Beaver on his tricycle. That sort of thing.

But Beaver was so preoccupied with his troubles with Larry that the next day he forgot to ask his mother for a baby picture to take to school for the carnival. Each day he told himself he would remember and each day he forgot because by now he was trying to think of a way to start speaking to Larry. He felt as if he wanted to speak to Larry more than anything in the whole world. He would just walk into school one morning and say, "Hi, Larry" as if nothing had happened. No, he better not do that. By now he could no longer be sure Larry was going to speak to *him*. It would really be bad if he spoke and Larry didn't speak back. That would be starting the fight all over again and they never would get it untangled. Maybe if he followed Larry down the hall Larry might happen to drop his notebook and Beaver could pick it up and call out, "Hey, Larry, you dropped your notebook," and Larry would take it and say, "Gee, thanks, Beaver" and everything would be all right once more. Beaver did follow Larry down the hall a couple of times but Larry did not drop anything.

Larry, Beaver could see, was not exactly avoiding

him, but he wasn't going to help him out of his
predicament, either. And why should he? He had
tried to make up once and Beaver had refused.
Beaver thought unhappily of Larry's peace offering,
a bag of his best marbles, still lying on the dresser
at home. He had refused to even thank Larry, and
they were good marbles because Larry, surprisingly,
was one of the best marble players in school.

Each day some of the boys and girls remembered
to bring their baby pictures to school. Miss Landers
propped up some of the pictures on the chalk rail
one morning, but those who brought the pictures
were careful not to identify them. Everyone laughed
at the picture of one baby boy who was playing
with his bare toes.

"Everybody will guess my picture when I bring
it, because I was so cute," said Judy. "My mother
says I looked just like Shirley Temple."

"Shirley Temple is a grownup lady on television,"
someone pointed out. "She is as old as your mother."

Judy tossed her head. "Well, she didn't used to
be. She used to be a cute little girl just like me."

Whitey said he was afraid everybody would guess
his picture because his father was in it, too, so he
had drawn a moustache and whiskers on his father
to disguise him.

"What did you go and tell us for?" asked Gilbert.
"Now everybody will be able to guess which is
your picture."

Each day Beaver forgot to ask his mother for a
picture and each day Miss Landers reminded him.
Then Miss Landers appointed Larry and Whitey

⚫nd Angela to be the committee in charge of pin-
ning up the baby pictures in the booth the Dads'
Club would build for the carnival.

Larry's being on the committee gave Beaver an
idea.

He would remember for sure to ask his mother
for his picture and when he took it to school he
would hand it to Larry and say as if he had forgotten
he was not speaking, "Here is my picture for the
carnival booth." And Larry would say, "Thanks,
Beaver." And everything would be all right again.
Yes, the baby picture would be a good excuse.

That day after school when Beaver was in the
kitchen studying the contents of the refrigerator to
see what kind of a sandwich he could make for
himself, Mrs. Cleaver remarked, "By the way,
Beaver, I left one of your baby pictures in the
school office for Miss Landers today."

Beaver was astonished. He had never mentioned
the picture to his mother. "You did? How come you
knew about it?"

Mrs. Cleaver laughed. "Don't forget, Beaver, I am
a member of the PTA. We have been working on
the carnival plans for weeks."

"Oh . . . sure." Beaver was thinking that there
went his plan to hand his picture to Larry. He
helped himself to some salami and a jar of peanut
butter. "What picture did you take?" he asked, not
that he cared much.

"There are several copies of it in an envelope in
your father's desk," answered Mrs. Cleaver. "I didn't
give them all away when he had them taken. I

couldn't bear to part with them because you were such a darling baby."

"Me?" asked Beaver, stacking up the ingredients of his sandwich and going into his father's study to see what he looked like when he was such a darling baby. Probably bald and drooly like any other baby. He was inclined to agree with the boy who thought all babies looked alike.

Beaver found Wally in the study looking up something in the encyclopedia. He laid his sandwich on the desk blotter, opened the drawer and pulled out the brown envelope.

"What are you poking around in Dad's desk for?" Wally wanted to know.

"I just wanted to see a copy of the baby picture Mom took to school for the carnival," explained Beaver as he pulled the pictures out of the envelope. He stared at them stunned.

"Boy, oh boy!" exclaimed Wally, looking over Beaver's shoulder. "Mom took *that* to school?"

"Yeah." Beaver continued to stare at the pictures, all five of them. There he was, a darling baby, his mother said, with a rattle in his hand, lying on his stomach on a white blanket *in his bare skin.* "Wally," he asked in a hushed voice, "how could anybody do this to a baby? A little old helpless baby that can't defend himself?" Boy! Just let anybody try to take a picture like that *now!*

Wally tried to make things seem much better by saying, "Well, gee, Beav—I've seen pictures like this in ads for talcum powder and stuff. They are in practically every magazine you pick up and I've even seen them on T.V."

"Yeah, but nobody knows who they are," Beaver pointed out, "and this is going to be put up in a PTA booth with my name on the back and all the kids are supposed to guess who it is." Beaver changed his opinion about all babies looking pretty much alike. Now he knew there were two kinds—babies with clothes on and babies with clothes off.

"Maybe nobody will guess who it is," suggested Wally and encouraged by this thought the boys studied the picture once more. "No," said Wally at last, "I think they will guess. You still look sort of like this."

"I do not!" Beaver was indignant, but the longer he looked at the picture, the more he thought Wally might be right. Even then he had a lot of dark hair that fell down over his forehead. And his face was the same shape. His nose wasn't quite so round, but his ears . . . Besides Whitey and Larry and Angela would have to know who it was and that was three people too many already. Why couldn't his mother have taken a snapshot of him riding a tricycle— anything but this one.

"But don't the other kids have baby pictures like this?" asked Wally.

"Of course not," said Beaver. "I've seen a bunch of them and they all had clothes on. There was one with bare feet and you should have heard the kids laughing at that. They made all kinds of dumb remarks about its little pinkies and I was sure glad that it wasn't my picture and now Mom takes something about a million times worse."

"Yeah, I know." Wally was sympathetic. "They're going to give you the business all right."

"Boy, am I going to tell Mom what she did to me!" said Beaver.

"Aw, you can't do that, Beaver," protested Wally. "There isn't anything wrong with the picture. It's just that the kids will make a big issue out of it."

"Yeah." Beaver had to admit Wally was right. There really was nothing wrong with the picture, except . . . he didn't have any clothes on and no boy would want his whole class to see his bare skin even if it was a long time ago.

"Besides," continued Wally, "Mom had these pictures taken and she thinks they're cute. You don't want to hurt her feelings, do you? She was just trying to help you out. Golly, I can remember when you got your first haircut. Mom cried."

"She did?" Beaver thought this was a strange thing to cry about.

"Yeah," said Wally. "I guess mothers are funny about some things like first haircuts and baby pictures. She still has a lock of your baby hair tied with a little blue bow."

Grudgingly Beaver admitted there were some things women just didn't understand. "Who do you think took the picture, Wally?"

Wally examined one of the pictures. "It says on the back 'Jean's Photo Studio.'"

"I sure hope Jean wasn't a lady," said Beaver. "What do you think I can do?"

"Search me," said Wally. "Try to get the picture back, I guess."

Beaver began to wonder if there was some way he could get his hands on the picture before Miss Landers gave it to the committee. He picked up his sandwich and went back into the kitchen. "Say, Mom, did you put that picture in an envelope when you took it to school?" he asked.

"Why, yes, Beaver. I wrote your name on the back and put it in an envelope and wrote 'In care of Miss Landers' on it," answered his mother. "Why?"

"Nothing," answered Beaver. "I just wondered." At least the picture was in an envelope. That might help. And Miss Landers might give it to Whitey or Angela. In that case he could just ask for the envelope back and say his mother had sent the wrong picture.

"Uh . . . Mom? How did you happen to choose that picture?" Beaver asked, thinking of the album full of snapshots of him with clothes on.

"It was such a nice clear picture," answered his mother. "Much clearer than any of the snapshots."

The next morning, the morning of the carnival, Beaver was the first one off the school bus and the first one into the classroom. "Uh . . . Miss Landers," he began even though he was out of breath. "Uh . . . did you get that baby picture my mother left in the office yesterday."

"Why, yes, Beaver," Miss Landers answered with a smile.

"Did you . . . uh . . . look at it?" It wouldn't be quite so bad to have Miss Landers see Beaver in his bare skin, but Beaver would just as soon she didn't.

"Why, no, I didn't," said Miss Landers. "I opened the envelope and saw your name on the back. I didn't look at the picture because I might want to try guessing and win a yo-yo too."

"Uh . . . where is it now?" asked Beaver.

"Why, I turned it over to someone on the committee. Larry, I think," said Miss Landers. "Why?"

"I just . . . wanted to make sure . . . it got there," said Beaver.

"You don't have a thing to worry about," said Miss Landers.

That's what she thinks, thought Beaver gloomily as he flopped into his seat. He had plenty to worry about. Plenty. Just wait till the class . . . the whole school saw his picture. And everybody would notice it the very first thing because he would be the only baby there with no clothes on and they would guess who he was right away because even with his clothes on he still looked a lot like his baby picture. The boys would have to make a lot of smart remarks about his dimples and how cute he looked, but the girls, or anyway, most of them except Judy, would be too embarrassed to say anything right out loud but they would go off in bunches and giggle the way girls do. There was one good thing. He wouldn't have to listen to a lot of old girls making remarks about his baby picture even though he would have to listen to their giggles and try to guess what they were saying. Come to think of it, maybe that would be worse.

Beaver did not do very well in school that day. Miss Landers had to remind him several times that even though this was the day of the P.T.A. carnival, the carnival did not begin until after school and in the meantime he must keep his mind on his work. She knew he was excited, but he came to school to learn. . . . Excited! thought Beaver, that was all Miss Landers knew about it.

When Larry and Gilbert and Angela were excused from class to go work in the booth, Beaver looked dolefully after them. He only hoped they would pin his picture way down at the bottom someplace, but knowing the way Larry felt toward him, it would be right smack in the middle where everyone would see it the first thing and laugh. Maybe Larry would even put a ruffle of crepe paper around—not that he would need to. It would attract enough attention all by itself. Well, he was in no hurry to see it. Maybe he wouldn't even go to the carnival. Maybe he would go home all by himself and read a book.

Beaver wished he had not been so stubborn about making up with Larry. He had been lonesome during the last weeks and now he sat at his desk thinking of all the good times he and Larry used to have going to the movies or not doing much of anything. He remembered the fun they had fooling Benjie with their magic trick and how they laughed the time they experimented with Wally's hair goo.

Everybody had a fight once in a while, and as Wally would say, why make a big thing of it? Beaver and Wally had had a fight over the hair goo and over Beaver's tagging along on the Igloo Bar route but they got over it. They both thought it was funny now. Well, it was Beaver who had made a big thing out of his fight with Larry and now he was stuck with it. He could not find a way out.

When school was finally over the class rushed out to the playground that was edged with booths made colorful with crepe paper. Music came over a loud-speaker and everyone seemed to be running and shouting and laughing. Everyone but Beaver who started home alone.

Then Whitey called after him. "Come on, Beav, let's be the first ones to throw baseballs at Mr. Grover."

Mr. Grover, the physical education teacher, had volunteered to put on a football helmet, poke his head through a hole in the blanket and let the boys try to hit him with a baseball, three shots for a dime. Of course Beaver was tempted. He would throw three balls and then go home. He went with Whitey and actually did hit Mr. Grover on the helmet with one of the baseballs.

Mr. Grover said, "Good shot. I see you can pitch as well as bat."

That cheered Beaver up so much that he looked around to see which of the booths he could take in without going near the baby-picture-guessing booth. A taffy apple seemed like a good investment and so did three shots at a lighted candle with a water pistol.

"Hey, come on, Beav," said Whitey when he had succeeded in dousing the candle with the water pistol, "Let's go see our booth."

"Aw, who wants to look at a bunch of old baby

pictures?" grumbled Beaver and took a big bite of his taffy apple.

"I do," said Whitey. "Come on."

Beaver could not help being curious about the display of baby pictures. He followed Whitey to the booth which was trimmed with garlands of red and white crepe paper. The pictures were tacked up on a bulletin board in the center. Each picture was numbered and boys and girls were writing down the numbers and the names of the people they thought the picture to be. Gilbert and Angela were on duty handing out papers and collecting dimes. Larry was standing beside the box of yo-yos that were given as prizes.

Beaver stood on the edge of the crowd and listened to the remarks being made.

"I'll bet that is Judy that one with a bunch of curls. She's always talking about how she looked like Shirley Temple."

"It can't be. That baby is cute and you know what Judy looks like."

"That one asleep with his face in a bowl of mush must be Larry."

"Yeah, he was a funny-looking baby."

"I was not!" said Larry. "My mother said I looked just like my grandmother."

"That's what I mean—a baby that looks like a grandmother is a funny-looking baby."

"Well—" said Larry, "it is better than looking like a baboon. Anyway, you aren't supposed to tell everyone who you think the pictures are. You're supposed to write it down."

Nobody was saying anything about a baby with no clothes on. Beaver moved closer. There was a lot of laughter and whispering and giggling. Now that he had come this far, he had to find out if he was the cause of it.

"Hey, I know who that is," exclaimed Judy, "That one over at the side must be Beav—"

"Sh-h-h," said Larry. "Don't tell everybody. If everybody guesses all the pictures we won't have enough prizes. We are supposed to make money, not go broke.'"

"Everybody will guess that one," said Judy. "It looks just like him. He was an awfully cute baby. His mother should have sent him to Hollywood like my mother was going to send me only she didn't."

Beaver gathered his courage together and looked. He expected to find his picture the first thing because he would be the only baby with no clothes. He glanced quickly over the bulletin board. All the babies seemed to be fully clothed. Perhaps his picture had been mislaid. Larry was always losing things. Maybe he had lost Beaver's picture—Beaver hoped.

"Aw, I'm not even there," Beaver said to Judy.

"You are, too. It looks exactly like you." Judy pointed to one of the smaller pictures.

Beaver stared at the little picture. Yes, it was his face, the very same face with his hair down over his forehead that was on the picture he had seen in his father's study, but the part with all that bare skin was missing. Beaver looked closer. There was no white margin around the picture and the edges were not quite straight. Someone had cut away the part of the picture he did not want anyone to see!

"Hey, Larry," said Beaver completely forgetting that he was not speaking, "Is that the picture of me that Miss Landers gave you?" Then, remembering that he was not speaking to Larry, he turned red. Others must have remembered, too, because there was a sudden silence. Then someone laughed.

"Yeah . . . sh-h," whispered Larry, beckoning Beaver away from the crowd. "I suppose your mother is going to be sore at me, but I cut off part of the picture because you didn't have any clothes on."

"Gee, Larry!" exclaimed Beaver gratefully. "Thanks. Thanks a lot! And don't worry about my mother. She has a whole stack of those pictures at home."

"That's good." Obviously Larry had been worried about cutting up someone else's picture. "I sure didn't want her to be mad at me, but golly, I wouldn't put up my worst enemy's picture looking like that. Why, all the kids would laugh themselves sick."

Beaver was reminded once more of the quarrel. "I—I guess I am your worst enemy," he said. "But thanks for helping me out anyway."

"Aw, gee, Beaver," protested Larry, "I didn't mean it that way."

"But you said 'your worst enemy,'" Beaver pointed out.

"That's just an expression," said Larry. "You know, like saying somebody looked like something the cat dragged in."

"Then I'm not your worst enemy?" asked Beaver hopefully.

"Shucks, no," said Larry. "I didn't blame you for getting sore at me after what I did, but I figured you shouldn't stay sore at me so long."

"You know," said Beaver thoughtfully, "that's what I got to thinking, too, but once a fellow starts being sore, sometimes he doesn't know how to stop."

"Yeah, I know, but I guess everybody gets mad at somebody once in a while," agreed Larry as if the subject was really not very important to him. "How about me treating you to a taffy apple? I'll get Whitey to hand out the yo-yos."

"Sure, Larry," said Beaver who had just eaten one taffy apple but was only too happy to join Larry in a second. As they left the baby-picture booth, he glanced back at his picture. Now he didn't care how many people guessed his picture. Besides, Judy was right. He had been a cute baby—now that just his head showed. "By the way, Larry, thanks for the . . . uh, marbles." He felt better now that he had said it.

"That's O.K.," answered Larry. "It won't take me long to win them back."

Made in the USA
Coppell, TX
01 April 2021